PRAISE FOR ALAN BENNETT

"Sharp . . . [*The Clothes They Stood Up In* is] a happy evening's
read and a tantalizing mental challenge to those
of us who, like the Ransomes, find their lives encumbered
and their senses blunted by too much stuff."
—BROOKE ALLEN, *The New York Times Book Review*

"Handsomely written and sneakily funny . . . [*The Clothes They
Stood Up In*] is a book of many more levels of meaning than
first impression might suggest."
—JONATHAN YARDLEY, *The Washington Post Book World*

"[*The Clothes They Stood Up In*] is always
charming and often hilarious."
—RON CHARLES, *The Christian Science Monitor*

"Few write sharper dialogue or probe more tellingly into the
frailties and occasional strengths of the human psyche than
Alan Bennett. None know more about getting each scene
just right or is as consistently witty."
—WILLIAM TREVOR

"[*The Clothes They Stood Up In* is] charmingly subversive. . . .
Bennett carries off his terse, surreal
comedy with witty aplomb."
—*Publishers Weekly*

" 'The Lady in the Van' will be remembered as one of the
finest bursts of comic writing the twentieth century has pro-
duced. The diary's narrative mixes, in equal parts, hilarity and
charity. . . . Bennett's pyrotechnic self-deprecation serves only
to widen the reach of both his comedy and his compassion."
—ROB NIXON, *The Village Voice*

"[In 'The Lady in the Van,'] Bennett displays wry humor
and profound sensitivity as he confronts the human
condition with surprising accuracy."
—*Booklist*

ALAN BENNETT is Britain's best-loved playwright. He first appeared on the stage in the revue *Beyond the Fringe*, which opened in London in 1961 and later transferred to Broadway. His subsequent stage plays include *Forty Years On, Habeas Corpus, The Old Country,* and *Kafka's Dick,* and his adaptation of *The Wind in the Willows,* the double bill *Single Spies,* and *The Madness of George III* were all presented at the Royal National Theatre. He has written many television plays, notably *An Englishman Abroad* and the two series of *Talking Heads* monologues. *Writing Home,* a collection of diaries and prose, was published by Random House in 1995. It included "The Lady in the Van," which he later adapted for the stage. It was presented in the West End with Maggie Smith in the leading role.

Through his many recordings of children's classics, Alan Bennett is one of the most familiar voices on BBC radio. He also writes regularly in the *London Review of Books.*

Also by Alan Bennett

Plays

Plays One (*Forty Years On, Getting On,
Habeas Corpus, Enjoy*)
Plays Two (*Kafka's Dick, The Insurance Man,
The Old Country, An Englishman Abroad,
A Question of Attribution*)

Office Suite
The Wind in the Willows
The Madness of George III
The Lady in the Van

Television plays

The Writer in Disguise
Objects of Affection (BBC)
Talking Heads (BBC)

Screenplays

A Private Function
Prick Up Your Ears
The Madness of King George

Autobiography

Writing Home

The Clothes They Stood Up In

AND

The Lady in the Van

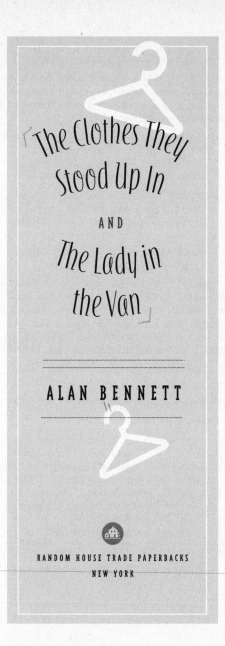

The Clothes They
Stood Up In

AND

The Lady in
the Van

ALAN BENNETT

RANDOM HOUSE TRADE PAPERBACKS
NEW YORK

2002 Random House Trade Paperback Edition

The Clothes They Stood Up In, originally published in the *London Review of Books,* was first published in book form in Great Britain by Profile Books Ltd., London, in 1998, and in the United States by Random House, Inc., in 2001. "The Lady in the Van" appeared in *Writing Home,* first published in Great Britain by Faber & Faber Limited, London, in 1994, and in the United States by Random House, Inc., in 1995.

Library of Congress Cataloging-in-Publication Data

Bennett, Alan.
The clothes they stood up in ; and, The lady in the van / Alan Bennett.
p. cm.
ISBN 0-8129-6965-0 *ISBN 0812. 966 430*
1. Middle aged persons—Fiction. 2. London (England)—Fiction.
3. Married people—Fiction. 4. Burglary—Fiction. 5. Bennett, Alan—
Friends and associates. 6. Eccentrics and eccentricities—England—
London. 7. Homeless women—England—London. I. Title: Clothes
they stood up in ; and, The lady in the van. II. Bennett, Alan. Lady in
the van. III. Title: Lady in the van. IV. Title.
PR6052.E5 C57 2002
823'.914—dc21   2002021360

Random House website address: www.atrandom.com

Printed in the United States of America

24689753

Book design by Barbara M. Bachman

Contents

INTRODUCTION IX

The Clothes They Stood Up In · 1

The Lady in the Van · 133

Introduction

One fact, the other fiction, "The Lady in the Van" and *The Clothes They Stood Up In* may seem an odd pairing, with the only link between them their author. Both narratives, it's true, feature a strong female protagonist (though Mrs. Ransome, the heroine of *The Clothes They Stood Up In*, would not think of herself as strong), and each is coping with an ineffectual man, Mrs. Ransome with her husband, Miss Shepherd with myself.

Since one of these women lives frugally in a van and the other has been burgled so comprehensively that she is left with only the clothes she stands up in, it would be natural to suspect that implicit in this coupling something is being said about possessions or the want of them.

I'm not sure, though, that this is the case. It's true that losing all her belongings does result in Mrs. Ransome becoming more of a free spirit, but the corollary of this—namely that, having few possessions, Miss Shepherd is a free spirit already—is far from being the case. No one was more rigid and censorious in her social and political views, a lack of worldly goods doing nothing to dispose her towards a liberal point of view or a tolerant attitude to her fellow creatures.

Nor is it true that Miss Shepherd set no store by the things of this world. Of course, living in the van she had few creature comforts and room for very little in the way of material possessions, but this did not stop her accumulating a whole fleet of vehicles of one sort or another, including (over the course of fifteen years) three vans, a three-wheeler car, an Austin Mini, two wheelchairs (one of which she used, the other a spare in case that "conked out"), and at least five children's pushchairs. And, if we are talking aids to locomotion, at least six (identical) walking sticks. Divesting herself of material encumbrances was never part of Miss Shepherd's scheme of things, and insofar as she had a final goal in life it was not general piety, peace of mind, or purity of spirit but the acquisition of yet another wheelchair, this one battery-powered, with which she tirelessly badgered the social services to endow her.

Still, living in the van, her only possessions what she could cram into it and clad in the first garment that came to hand and always unwashed, Miss Shepherd might seem to embody an alternative lifestyle. This was not how she saw it. No matter that she was kitted out in an ancient raincoat over a dress run up out of some old curtains, her shoes a run-down pair of men's carpet slippers and on her head a sun hat made out of a chiffon scarf tied round part of a cornflakes packet, the picture she had of herself was of a bona fide member of the middle class . . . poor, possibly, but not derelict and certainly not a tramp.

Our street was home to several redoubtable women: the widow of the composer Ralph Vaughan Williams, the wife of the author V. S. Pritchett, the ex-wife of the novelist Kingsley Amis. It was to this substantial and self-assured sisterhood that Miss Shepherd saw herself as belonging.

In "The Lady in the Van" and *The Clothes They Stood Up In*, both women come to a crossroads—Miss Shepherd quite literally, as it was there that the motor-cyclist met his death under the van. But whereas the burglary that alters Mrs. Ransome's life inaugurates her emancipation and a change for the better, I can't claim that this symmetry was in my mind when, some years after "The Lady in the Van," I wrote *The Clothes They Stood Up In*. I would have said at that time that Mrs. Ransome's dreams of leaving and her need to capitalize on the loss of her possessions in order to lead a different life were an echo of the longings of my mother, who dreamed much of "branching out" (as she put it) and becoming a different and more outgoing woman.

That Miss Shepherd clung to dreams, too, I realized when in clearing out the van after her death I came across a set of kitchen implements (spatula, straining spoon, potato masher) mounted on a bracket that was meant to be hung on a kitchen wall. Still in their original packaging, these model implements could never have been used, still less mounted in the van, but must have represented for this ramshackle, unhousewifely woman a vision of suburban order, trim and hygienic, that was waiting for her when her van days were done.

The big difference between the two women in this book is that Mrs. Ransome is altogether nicer and kinder than Miss Shepherd. Indeed, I would have found it hard to invent a character so utterly wanting in humanity as Miss Shepherd, and though in the end I came to delight in her demonstrations of unfeeling and to see in them the triumph of an indomitable spirit, I never learned just to shrug them off.

In my first play, *Forty Years On,* there is a parody of *The Importance of Being Earnest* in which a Lady Bracknell figure is pushed on in a wheelchair. Abruptly she rises, airily dismissing the wheelchair with the words "I can walk. It's just that I'm so rich I don't need to." Miss Shepherd could always walk, too, but towards the end she began to look so poor and decrepit that she didn't need to either, and if she stationed herself outside my gate in her chair, some kindly soul would invariably push her down the street to the market, where he or she would then be dismissed, their kindness unacknowledged and always unthanked.

In the stage play of "The Lady in the Van," Miss Shepherd ends up, still in the van, ascending into heaven. Mrs. Ransome's visit to the penthouse is an ascent into heaven, too, where she meets if not God, at least an angel, in an encounter which explains how the comprehensive burglary which begins the book has come about.

Miss Shepherd saw heavenly beings, too . . . the Virgin waiting at the bus stop round the corner or dressed as Queen Victoria and hovering over the convent at the top of the street. Her workaday funeral did not lend itself to poetry, but her piety, her intransigence, and her unrest might have been fittingly commemorated in the words of another devout and derelict Catholic, Francis Thompson:

> But (when so sad thou canst not sadder)
> Cry,—and upon thy so sore loss
> Shall shine the traffic of Jacob's ladder
> Pitched betwixt Heaven and Charing Cross
>
> Yea, in the night, my Soul, my daughter,
> Cry,—clinging Heaven by the hems;
> And lo, Christ walking on the water
> Not of Gennesareth, but Thames!

Alan Bennett
February 2002

The Clothes They Stood Up In

The Ransomes had been burgled. "Robbed," Mrs. Ransome said. "Burgled," Mr. Ransome corrected. Premises were burgled; persons were robbed. Mr. Ransome was a solicitor by profession and thought words mattered. Though "burgled" was the wrong word too. Burglars select; they pick; they remove one item and ignore others. There is a limit to what burglars can take: they seldom take easy chairs, for example, and even more seldom settees. These burglars did. They took everything.

The Ransomes had been to the opera, to *Così fan tutte* (or *Così* as Mrs. Ransome had learned to call it). Mozart played an important part in their marriage. They had no children and but for Mozart would probably have split up years ago. Mr. Ransome always took a bath when he came home from work and then he had his supper. After supper he took another bath, this time in Mozart. He wallowed in Mozart; he luxuriated in him; he let the little Viennese soak away all the dirt and disgustingness he had had to sit through in his office all day. On this particular evening he had been to the public baths, Covent Garden, where their seats were immediately behind the Home Secretary. He too was taking a bath and washing away the cares of his day, cares, if only in the form of a statistic, that were about to include the Ransomes.

On a normal evening, though, Mr. Ransome shared his bath with no one, Mozart coming personalized via his headphones and a stack of complex and finely balanced stereo equipment that Mrs. Ransome was never allowed to touch. She blamed the stereo for the burglary as that was what the robbers were probably after in the first place. The theft of stereos is common; the theft of fitted carpets is not.

"Perhaps they wrapped the stereo in the carpet," said Mrs. Ransome.

Mr. Ransome shuddered and said her fur coat was more likely, whereupon Mrs. Ransome started crying again.

It had not been much of a *Così*. Mrs. Ransome could not follow the plot and Mr. Ransome, who never tried, found the performance did not compare with the four recordings he possessed of the work. The acting he invariably found distracting. "None of them knows what to do with their arms," he said to his wife in the interval. Mrs. Ransome thought it probably went further than their arms but did not say so. She was wondering if the casserole she had left in the oven would get too dry at Gas Mark 4. Perhaps 3 would have been better. Dry it may well have been but there was no need to have worried. The thieves took the oven and the casserole with it.

The Ransomes lived in an Edwardian block of flats the color of ox blood not far from Regent's Park. It was handy for the City, though Mrs. Ransome would have preferred something farther out, seeing herself with a trug in a garden, vaguely. But she was not gifted in that direction. An African violet that her cleaning lady had given her at Christmas had finally given up the ghost that very morning and she had been forced to hide it in the wardrobe out of Mrs. Clegg's way. More wasted effort. The wardrobe had gone too.

They had no neighbors to speak of, or seldom to. Occasionally they ran into people in the lift and both parties would smile cautiously. Once they had asked some newcomers on their floor around to sherry, but he had turned out to be what he called "a big band freak" and she had been a dental receptionist with a timeshare in Portugal, so one way and another it had been an awkward evening and they had never repeated the experience. These days the turnover of tenants seemed increasingly rapid and the lift more and more wayward. People were always moving in and out again, some of them Arabs.

"I mean," said Mrs. Ransome, "it's getting like a hotel."

"I wish you wouldn't keep saying 'I mean,'" said Mr. Ransome. "It adds nothing to the sense."

He got enough of what he called "this sloppy way of talking" at work; the least he could ask for at home, he felt, was correct English. So Mrs. Ransome, who normally had very little to say, now tended to say even less.

When the Ransomes had moved into Naseby Mansions the flats boasted a commissionaire in a plum-colored uniform that matched the color of the building. He had died one afternoon in 1982 as he was hailing a taxi for Mrs. Brabourne on the second floor, who had forgone it in order to let it take him to hospital. None of his successors had shown the same zeal in office or pride in the uniform and eventually the function of commissionaire had merged with that of the caretaker, who was never to be found on the door and seldom to be found anywhere, his lair a hot scullery behind the boiler room where he slept much of the day in an armchair that had been thrown out by one of the tenants.

On the night in question the caretaker was asleep, though unusually for him not in the armchair but at the theater. On the lookout for a classier type of girl he had decided to attend an adult education course where he had opted to study English; given the opportunity, he had told the lecturer, he would like to become a voracious reader. The lecturer had some exciting though not very well formulated ideas about art and the workplace, and learning he was a caretaker had got him tickets for the play of the same name, thinking the resultant insights would be a stimulant to group interaction. It was an evening the caretaker found no more satisfying than the Ransomes did *Così* and the insights he gleaned limited: "So far as your actual caretaking was concerned," he reported to the class, "it was bollocks." The lecturer consoled himself with the hope that, unknown to the caretaker, the evening might have opened doors. In this he was right: the doors in question belonged to the Ransomes' flat.

The police came around eventually, though there was more to it than picking up the phone. The thieves had done that anyway, all three phones in fact, neatly snipping off the wire flush with the skirting board so that, with no answer from the flat opposite ("Sharing time in Portugal, probably," Mr. Ransome said, "or at a big band concert"), he was forced to sally forth in search of a phone box. "No joke," as he said to Mrs. Ransome now that phone boxes doubled as public conveniences. The first two Mr. Ransome tried didn't even do that, urinals solely, the phone long since ripped out. A mobile would have been the answer, of course, but Mr. Ransome had resisted this innovation ("Betrays a lack of organization"), as he resisted most innovations except those in the sphere of stereophonic reproduction.

He wandered on through deserted streets, wondering how people managed. The pubs had closed, the only place open a launderette with, in the window, a pay phone. This struck Mr. Ransome as a stroke of luck; never having had cause to use such an establishment he had not realized that washing clothes ran to such a facility; but being new to launderettes meant also that he was not certain if someone who was not actually washing clothes was permitted to take advantage of it. However, the phone was currently being used by the sole occupant of the place, an old lady in two overcoats who had plainly not laundered her clothes in some time, so Mr. Ransome took courage.

She was standing with the phone pressed to her dirty ear, not talking, but not really listening either.

"Could you hurry, please," Mr. Ransome said. "This is an emergency."

"So is this, dear," said the woman. "I'm calling Padstow, only they're not answering."

"I want to call the police," said Mr. Ransome.

"Been attacked, have you?" said the woman. "I was

attacked last week. It's par for the course these days. He was only a toddler. It's ringing but there's a long corridor. They tend to have a hot drink about this time. They're nuns," she said explanatorily.

"Nuns?" said Mr. Ransome. "Are you sure they won't have gone to bed?"

"No. They're up and down all night having the services. There's always somebody about."

She went on listening to the phone ringing in Cornwall.

"Can't it wait?" asked Mr. Ransome, seeing his effects halfway up the M1. "Speed is of the essence."

"I know," said the old lady, "whereas nuns have got all the time in the world. That's the beauty of it except when it comes to answering the phone. I aim to go on retreat there in May."

"But it's only February," Mr. Ransome said. "I . . ."

"They get booked up," explained the old lady. "There's no talking and three meals a day so do you wonder? They use it as a holiday home for religious of both sexes. You wouldn't think nuns needed holidays. Prayer doesn't take it out of you. Not like bus conducting. Still ringing. They've maybe finished their hot drink and adjourned to the chapel. I suppose I could ring later, only . . ." She looked at the coins waiting in Mr. Ransome's hand. "I've put my money in now."

Mr. Ransome gave her a pound and she took the other 50p besides, saying, "You don't need money for 999."

She put the receiver down and her money came back of its own accord, but Mr. Ransome was so anxious to get on with his call he scarcely noticed. It was only later, sitting on the floor of what had been their bedroom, that he said out loud, "Do you remember Button A and Button B? They've gone, you know. I never noticed."

"Everything's gone," said Mrs. Ransome, not catching his drift, "the air freshener, the soap dish. They can't be human; I mean they've even taken the lavatory brush."

"Fire, police, or ambulance?" said a woman's voice.

"Police," said Mr. Ransome. There was a pause.

"I feel better for that banana," said a man's voice. "Yes? Police." Mr. Ransome began to explain but the man cut him short. "Anyone in danger?" He was chewing.

"No," said Mr. Ransome, "but . . ."

"Any threat to the person?"

"No," said Mr. Ransome, "only . . ."

"Slight bottleneck at the moment, chief," said the voice. "Bear with me while I put you on hold."

Mr. Ransome found himself listening to a Strauss waltz.

"They're probably having a hot drink," said the old lady, who he could smell was still at his elbow.

"Sorry about that," the voice said five minutes later.

"We're on manual at the moment. The computer's got hiccups. How may I help you?"

Mr. Ransome explained there had been a burglary and gave the address.

"Are you on the phone?"

"Of course," said Mr. Ransome, "only . . ."

"And the number is?"

"They've taken the phone," said Mr. Ransome.

"Nothing new there," said the voice. "Cordless job?"

"No," said Mr. Ransome. "One was in the sitting room, one was by the bed. . . ."

"We don't want to get bogged down in detail," said the voice. "Besides, the theft of a phone isn't the end of the world. What was the number again?"

It was after one o'clock when Mr. Ransome got back and Mrs. Ransome, already beginning to pick up the threads, was in what had been their bedroom, sitting with her back to the wall in the place where she would have been in bed had there been a bed to be in. She had done a lot of crying while Mr. Ransome was out but had now wiped her eyes, having decided she was going to make the best of things.

"I thought you might be dead," she said.

"Why dead?"

"Well, it never rains but it pours."

"I was in one of these launderettes if you want to know. It was terrible. What are you eating?"

"A cough sweet. I found it in my bag." This was one of the sweets Mr. Ransome insisted she take with her whenever they went to the opera ever since she had had a snuffle all the way through *Fidelio*.

"Is there another?"

"No," said Mrs. Ransome, sucking. "This is the last."

Mr. Ransome went to the lavatory, only realizing when it was too late that the burglary had been so comprehensive as to have taken in both the toilet roll and its holder.

"There's no paper," called Mrs. Ransome.

The only paper in the flat was the program from *Così* and passing it around the door Mrs. Ransome saw, not without satisfaction, that Mr. Ransome was going to have to wipe his bottom on a picture of Mozart.

Both unwieldy and unyielding the glossy brochure (sponsored by Barclays Bank PLC) was uncomfortable to use and unsinkable afterwards, and three flushes notwithstanding, the fierce eye of Sir Georg Solti still came squinting resentfully around the bend of the pan.

"Better?" said Mrs. Ransome.

"No," said her husband and settled down beside her against the wall. However, finding the skirting board dug into her back Mrs. Ransome changed her position to lie at right angles to her husband so that her head now rested on his thigh, a situation it had not been in for many a long year. While telling himself this was an emergency it was a conjunction Mr. Ransome found both uncomfortable and embarrassing, but which seemed to suit his wife as she straightaway went off to sleep, leaving Mr. Ransome staring glumly at the wall opposite and its now uncurtained window, from which, he noted wonderingly, the burglars had even stolen the curtain rings.

It was four o'clock before the police arrived, a big middle-aged man in a raincoat, who said he was a detective sergeant, and a sensitive-looking young constable in uniform, who didn't say anything at all.

"You've taken your time," said Mr. Ransome.

"Yes," said the sergeant. "We would have been earlier but there was a slight . . . ah, glitch as they say. Rang the wrong doorbell. The fault of mi-laddo here. Saw the name Hanson and . . ."

"No," said Mr. Ransome. "Ransome."

"Yes. We established that . . . eventually. Just moved in, have you?" said the sergeant, surveying the bare boards.

"No," said Mr. Ransome. "We've been here for thirty years."

"Fully furnished, was it?"

"Of course," said Mr. Ransome. "It was a normal home."

"A settee, easy chairs, a clock," said Mrs. Ransome. "We had everything."

"Television?" said the constable, timidly.

"Yes," said Mrs. Ransome.

"Only we didn't watch it much," said Mr. Ransome.

"Video recorder?"

"No," said Mr. Ransome. "Life's complicated enough."

"CD player?"

"Yes," said Mrs. Ransome and Mr. Ransome together.

"And my wife had a fur coat," said Mr. Ransome. "My insurers have a list of the valuables."

"In that case," said the sergeant, "you are laughing. I'll just have a little wander round if you don't mind, while Constable Partridge takes down the details. People opposite see the intruder?"

"Away in Portugal," said Mr. Ransome.

"Caretaker?"

"Probably in Portugal too," said Mr. Ransome, "for all we see of him."

"Is it Ransom as in king's?" said the constable. "Or Ransome as in Arthur?"

"Partridge is one of our graduate entrants," said the sergeant, examining the front door. "Lock not forced, I see. He's just climbing the ladder. There wouldn't be such a thing as a cup of tea, would there?"

"No," said Mr. Ransome shortly, "because there wouldn't be such a thing as a teapot. Not to mention a tea bag to put in it."

"I take it you'll want counseling," said the constable.

"What?"

"Someone comes along and holds your hand," said the sergeant, looking at the window. "Partridge thinks it's important."

"We're all human," said the constable.

"I'm a solicitor," said Mr. Ransome.

"Well," said the sergeant, "perhaps your missus could give it a try. We like to keep Partridge happy."

Mrs. Ransome smiled helpfully.

"I'll put yes," said the constable.

"They didn't leave anything behind, did they?" asked the sergeant, sniffing and reaching up to run his hand along the picture-rail.

"No," said Mr. Ransome testily. "Not a thing. As you can see."

"I didn't mean something of yours," said the sergeant. "I meant something of theirs." He sniffed again, inquiringly. "A calling card."

"A calling card?" said Mrs. Ransome.

"Excrement," said the sergeant. "Burglary is a nervous business. They often feel the need to open their bowels when doing a job."

"Which is another way of saying it, sergeant," said the constable.

"Another way of saying what, Partridge?"

"Doing a job is another way of saying opening the bowels. In France," said the constable, "it's known as posting a sentry."

"Oh, teach you that at Leatherhead, did they?" said the sergeant. "Partridge is a graduate of the police college."

"It's like a university," explained the constable, "only they don't have scarves."

"Anyway," said the sergeant, "have a scout around. For the excrement, I mean. They can be very creative about it. Burglary in Pangbourne I attended once where they done it halfway up the wall in an eighteenth-century light fitting. Any other sphere and they'd have got the Duke of Edinburgh's Award."

"You've perhaps not noticed," Mr. Ransome said grimly, "but we don't have any light fittings."

"Another one in Guildford did it in a bowl of this potpourri."

"That would be irony," said the constable.

"Oh would it?" said the sergeant. "And there was me thinking it was just some foul-assed, light-fingered little smackhead afflicted with incontinence. Still, while we're talking about bodily functions, before we take our leave I'll just pay a visit myself."

Too late Mr. Ransome realized he should have warned him and took refuge in the kitchen.

The sergeant came out shaking his head.

"Well, at least our friends had the decency to use the toilet but they've left it in a disgusting state. I never thought I'd have to do a Jimmy Riddle over Dame Kiri

Te Kanawa. Her recording of *West Side Story* is one of the gems of my record collection."

"To be fair," said Mrs. Ransome, "that was my husband."

"Dear me," said the sergeant.

"What was?" said Mr. Ransome, coming back into the room.

"Nothing," said his wife.

"Do you think you'll catch them?" said Mr. Ransome as he stood at the door with the two policemen.

The sergeant laughed.

"Well, miracles do happen, even in the world of law enforcement. Nobody got a grudge against you, have they?"

"I'm a solicitor," said Mr. Ransome. "It's possible."

"And it's not somebody's idea of a joke?"

"A *joke*?" said Mr. Ransome.

"Just a thought," said the sergeant. "But if it's your genuine burglar, I'll say this: he always comes back."

The constable nodded in sage confirmation; even Leatherhead was agreed on this. "Come back?" said Mr. Ransome bitterly, looking at the empty flat. *"Come back? What the fuck for?"*

Mr. Ransome seldom swore and Mrs. Ransome, who had stayed in the other room, pretended she hadn't heard. The door closed.

"Useless," said Mr. Ransome, coming back. "Utterly useless. It makes you want to swear."

"Well," said Mrs. Ransome a few hours later, "we shall just have to camp out. After all," she added not un-happily, "it could be fun."

"Fun?" said Mr. Ransome. *"Fun?"*

He was unshaven, unwashed, his bottom was sore and his breakfast had been a drink of water from the tap. Still, no amount of pleading on Mrs. Ransome's part could stop him going heroically off to work, with his wife instinctively knowing even in these unprecedented circumstances that her role was to make much of his self-less dedication.

Even so, when he'd gone and with the flat so empty, Mrs. Ransome missed him a little, wandering from room to echoing room not sure where she should start. Deciding to make a list she forgot for the moment she had nothing to make a list with and nothing to make a list on. This meant a visit to the newsagents for pad and pencil where, though she'd never noticed it before, she found there was a café next door. It seemed to be doing hot breakfasts, and, though in her opera clothes she felt a bit out of place among the taxi drivers and bicycle couriers who comprised most of the clientele, nobody took much notice of her, the waitress even calling her "duck" and offering her a copy of *The Mirror* to read while she waited for her bacon, egg, baked beans and fried bread. It wasn't a paper she would normally read, but bacon, egg, baked beans and fried bread wasn't a breakfast she would normally eat either, and she got so interested in the paper's tales of royalty and its misdemeanors that she propped it up against the sauce bottle so that she could read and eat, completely forgetting that one of the reasons she had come into the café was to make herself a list.

Wanting a list, her shopping was pretty haphazard. She went off to Boots first and bought some toilet rolls and some paper plates and cups, but she forgot soap. And when she remembered soap and went back for it, she forgot tea bags, and when she remembered tea bags, she forgot paper towels, until what with trailing halfway to the flats then having to go back again, she began to feel worn out.

It was on the third of these increasingly flustered trips (now having forgotten plastic cutlery) that Mrs. Ransome ventured into Mr. Anwar's. She had passed the shop many times as it was midway between the flats and St. John's Wood High Street; indeed she remembered it opening and the little draper's and babies' knitwear shop which it had replaced and where she had been a loyal customer. That had been kept by a Miss Dorsey, from whom over the years she had bought the occasional tray cloth or hank of Sylko but, on a much more regular basis, plain brown paper packets of what in those days were called "towels." The closing-down of the shop in the late sixties had left Mrs. Ransome anxious and unprotected and it came as a genuine surprise on venturing into Timothy White's to find that technology in this intimate department had lately made great strides that were unreflected in Miss Dorsey's ancient stock, of which Mrs. Ransome, as the last of a dwindling clientele, had been almost the sole consumer. She was old-fashioned, she knew that, but snobbery had come into it too, Mrs. Ransome feeling it vaguely classier to have her requirements passed wordlessly across the counter with Miss Dorsey's patient, suffering smile ("Our cross," it said) rather than taken from some promiscuous shelf in Timothy White's.

time to the High Street, she thought she might go in and ask if they had such a thing as boot polish (there were more pressing requirements, as she would have been the first to admit, only Mr. Ransome was very particular about his shoes). Though over twenty years had passed, the shop was still recognizably what it had been in Miss Dorsey's day because, other than having introduced a freezer and cold cupboards, Mr. Anwar had simply adapted the existing fixtures to his changed require-ments. Drawers that had previously been devoted to the genteel accoutrements of a leisured life—knitting pat-terns, crochet hooks, Rufflette—now housed nan and pita bread; spices replaced bonnets and booties; and the shelves and deep drawers that once were home to hosiery and foundation garments were now filled with rice and chickpeas.

Mrs. Ransome thought it unlikely they had polish in stock (did they wear normal shoes?), but she was weary enough to give it a try, though, since oxblood was what she wanted (or Mr. Ransome required), she thought vaguely it might be a shade to which they had religious objections. But plump and cheerful Mr. Anwar brought out several tins for her kind consideration and while she was paying she spotted a nailbrush they would be need-ing; then the tomatoes looked nice and there was a lemon, and while she was at it the shop seemed to sell hardware so she invested in a colander. As she wandered around the shop the normally tongue-tied Mrs. Ran-some found herself explaining to this plump and ami-able grocer the circumstances that had led her to the purchase of such an odd assortment of things. And he smiled and shook his head in sympathy while at the same time suggesting other items she would doubtless be needing to replace and that he would happily supply. "They cleaned you out of house and home, the blighters. You will not know whether you are coming or going. You will need washing-up liquid and one of these blocks to make the toilet a more savory place."

So she ended up buying a dozen or so items, too many for her to carry, but this didn't matter either as Mr. Anwar fetched his little boy from the flat upstairs (I hope I'm not dragging him away from the Koran, she thought) and he followed Mrs. Ransome home in his little white cap, carrying her shopping in a cardboard box.

"Seconds probably," said Mr. Ransome later. "That's how they make a profit."

Mrs. Ransome didn't quite see how there could be seconds in shoe polish but didn't say so.

"Hopefully," she said, "they'll deliver."

"You mean," said Mr. Ransome (and it was old ground), "you hope they'll deliver. 'Hopefully they'll deliver' means that deliveries are touch and go" (though that was probably true too).

"Anyway," said Mrs. Ransome defiantly, "he stays open till ten at night."

"He can afford to," said Mr. Ransome. "He probably pays no wages. I'd stick to Marks and Spencer."

Which she did, generally speaking. Though once she popped in and bought a mango for her lunch and another time a papaw; small adventures, it's true, but departures nevertheless, timorous voyages of discovery which she knew her husband well enough to keep to herself.

The Ransomes had few friends; they seldom entertained, Mr. Ransome saying that he saw quite enough of people at work. On the rare occasions when Mrs. Ransome ran into someone she knew and ventured to recount their dreadful experience she was surprised to find that everyone, it seemed, had their own burglar story. None, she felt, was so stark or so shocking as to measure up to theirs, which ought in fairness to have trumped outright these other less flamboyant break-ins, but comparison scarcely seemed to enter into it: the friends only endured her story as an unavoidable prelude to telling her their own. She asked Mr. Ransome if he had noticed this.

"Yes," he said shortly. "Anybody would think it happened every day."

Which, of course, it did but not, he was certain, as definitively, as out-and-outedly, as altogether epically as this.

"Everything," Mr. Ransome told Gail, his longtime secretary, "every single thing."

Gail was a tall, doleful-looking woman, which normally suited Mr. Ransome very well as he could not abide much of what he called "silliness"—i.e., femininity. Had Gail been a bit sillier, though, she might have been more sympathetic, but like everyone else she weighed in with a burglar story of her own, saying she was surprised it hadn't happened before as most people she knew had been burgled at least once and her brother-in-law, who was a chiropodist in Ilford, twice, one of which had been a ram-raid while they were watching television.

"What you have to watch out for is the trauma; it

takes people in different ways. Hair loss is often a con-
sequence of burglary apparently and my sister came out
in terrible eczema. Mind you," Gail went on, "it's always
men."

"Always men what?" said Mr. Ransome.

"Who burgle."

"Well, women shoplift," said Mr. Ransome defen-
sively.

"Not to that extent," said Gail. "They don't clean out
the store."

Not sure how he had ended up on the wrong side of
the argument, Mr. Ransome felt both irritated and dis-
satisfied, so he tried Mr. Pardoe from the firm next door
but with no more success. "Cleaned you out completely? Well, be grateful you weren't in. My dentist and
his wife were tied up for seven hours and counted themselves lucky not to be raped. Balaclavas, walkie-talkies.
It's an industry nowadays. I'd castrate them."

That night Mr. Ransome took out a dictionary from

his briefcase, both dictionary and briefcase newly acquired. The dictionary was Mr. Ransome's favorite book.

"What are you doing?" asked Mrs. Ransome.

"Looking up 'lock, stock and barrel.' I suppose it means the same as 'the whole shoot.' "

Over the next week or so Mrs. Ransome assembled the rudiments—two camp beds plus bedding, towels, a card table and two folding chairs. She bought a couple of what she called beanbags, though the shop called them something else; they were quite popular apparently, even among people who had not been burgled, who used them to sit on the floor by choice. There was even (this was Mr. Ransome's contribution) a portable CD player and a recording of *The Magic Flute*.

Mrs. Ransome had always enjoyed shopping so this obligatory re-equipment with the essentials of life was not without its pleasures, though the need was so pressing that choice scarcely entered into it. Hitherto anything electrical had always to be purchased by, or under the supervision of, Mr. Ransome, a sanction that applied even with an appliance like the vacuum cleaner, which he never wielded, or the dishwasher, which he seldom stacked. However, in the special circumstances obtaining after the burglary, Mrs. Ransome found herself licensed to buy whatever was deemed necessary, electrical or otherwise; not only did she get an electric kettle, she also went in for a microwave oven, an innovation Mr. Ransome had long resisted and did not see the point of.

That many of these items (the beanbags for instance) were likely to be discarded once the insurance paid out and they acquired something more permanent did not diminish Mrs. Ransome's quiet zest in shopping for them. Besides, the second stage was likely to be somewhat delayed as the insurance policy had been stolen too, together with all their other documents, so compensation, while not in doubt, might be slow in coming. In the meantime they lived a stripped-down sort of life which seemed to Mrs. Ransome, at least, not unpleasant.

"Hand to mouth," said Mr. Ransome.

"Living out of a suitcase," said Croucher, his insurance broker.

"No," said Mr. Ransome. "We don't have a suitcase."

"You don't think," asked Croucher, "it might be some sort of joke?"

"People keep saying that," said Mr. Ransome. "Jokes must have changed since my day. I thought they were meant to be funny."

"What sort of CD equipment was it?" said Croucher.

"Oh, state-of-the-art," said Mr. Ransome. "The latest and the best. I've got the receipts somewhere . . . oh no, of course. I was forgetting."

Though this was a genuine slip it was perhaps fortunate that the receipts had been stolen along with the equipment that they were for, because Mr. Ransome was telling a little lie. His sound equipment was not quite state-of-the-art, as what equipment is? Sound reproduction is not static; perfection is ongoing and scarcely a week passes without some technical advance. As an avid reader of hi-fi magazines, Mr. Ransome often saw advertised refinements he would dearly have liked to make part of his listening experience. The burglary, devastating though it had been, was his opportunity. So it was at the moment when he woke up to the potential advantages of his loss that this most unresilient of men began, if grudgingly, to bounce back.

Mrs. Ransome, too, could see the cheerful side of things, but then she always did. When they had got married they had kitted themselves out with all the necessities of a well-run household; they had a dinner service, a tea service plus table linen to match; they had dessert dishes and trifle glasses and cake stands galore. There were mats for the dressing table, coasters for the coffee table, runners for the dining table; guest towels with matching flannels for the basin, lavatory mats with matching ones for the bath. They had cake slices and fish slices and other slices besides, delicate trowels in silver and bone the precise function of which Mrs. Ransome had never been able to fathom. Above all there was a massive many-tiered canteen of cutlery, stocked with sufficient knives, forks and spoons for a dinner party for twelve. Mr. and Mrs. Ransome did not have dinner parties for twelve. They did not have dinner parties. They seldom used the guest towels because they never had guests. They had transported this paraphernalia with them across thirty-two years of marriage to no purpose at all that Mrs. Ransome could see, and now at a stroke they were rid of the lot. Without quite knowing why, and while she was washing up their two cups in the sink, Mrs. Ransome suddenly burst out singing.

"It's probably best," said Croucher, "to proceed on the assumption that it's gone and isn't going to come

abruptly parted from all her worldly goods might bring
with it benefits she would have hesitated to call spiritual
but which might, more briskly, be put under the heading
of "improving the character." To have the carpet almost
literally pulled from under her should, she felt, induce
salutary thoughts about the way she had lived her life.
War would once have rescued her, of course, some turn
of events that gave her no choice, and while what had
happened was not a catastrophe on that scale she knew
it was up to her to make of it what she could. She would
go to museums, she thought, art galleries, learn about
the history of London; there were classes in all sorts
nowadays—classes that she could perfectly well have
attended before they were deprived of everything they
had in the world, except that it was everything they had
in the world, she felt, that had been holding her back.
Now she could start. So, plumped down on the beanbag
on the bare boards of her sometime lounge, Mrs. Ransome found that she was not unhappy, telling herself

that this was more real and that (though one needed to be comfortable) an uncushioned life was the way they ought to live.

It was at this point that the doorbell rang.

"My name is Briscoe," the voice said over the intercom. "Your counselor?"

"We're Conservatives," said Mrs. Ransome.

"No," said the voice. "The police? Your trauma? The burglary?"

Knowing the counselor had come via the police Mrs. Ransome had expected someone a bit, well, crisper. There was nothing crisp about Ms. Briscoe, except possibly her name, and she got rid of that on the doorstep.

"No, no. Call me Dusty. Everybody does."

"Were you christened Dusty?" asked Mrs. Ransome, bringing her in. "Or is that just what you're called?"

"Oh no. My proper name is Brenda but I don't want to put people off."

Mrs. Ransome wasn't quite sure how, though it was true she didn't look like a Brenda; whether she looked like a Dusty she wasn't sure as she'd never met one before.

She was a biggish girl who, perhaps wisely, had opted for a smock rather than a frock and with it a cardigan so long and ample it was almost a dress in itself, one pocket stuffed with her diary and notebook, the other sagging under the weight of a mobile phone. Considering she worked for the authorities Mrs. Ransome thought Dusty looked pretty slapdash.

"Now you are Mrs. Ransome? Rosemary Ransome?"

"Yes."

"And that's what people call you, is it? Rosemary?"

"Well, yes." (Insofar as they call me anything, thought Mrs. Ransome.)

"Just wondered if it was Rose or Rosie?"

"Oh no."

"Hubby calls you Rosemary, does he?"

"Well, yes," said Mrs. Ransome, "I suppose he does," and went to put the kettle on, thus enabling Dusty to make her first note: "Query: Is burglary the real problem here?"

When Dusty had started out counseling, victims were referred to as "cases." That had long since gone; they were now "clients" or even "customers," terms Dusty to begin with found unsympathetic and had resisted. Nowadays she never gave either designation a second thought—what her clients were called seemed as immaterial as the disasters that befell them. Victims singled themselves out; be it burglary, mugging or road accidents, these mishaps were simply the means by which inadequate people came to her notice. And everybody given the chance had the potential to be inadequate. Experience, she felt, had turned her into a professional.

They took their tea into the sitting room and each

sank onto a beanbag, a maneuver Mrs. Ransome was now quite good at, though with Dusty it was more like a tumble. "Are these new?" said Dusty, wiping some tea from her smock. "I was with another client yesterday, the sister of someone who's in a coma, and she had something similar. Now, Rosemary, I want us to try and talk this through together."

Mrs. Ransome wasn't sure whether "talking this through" was the same as "talking it over." One seemed a more rigorous, less meandering version of the other, the difference in Dusty's choice of preposition not boding well for fruitful discourse. "More structured," Dusty would have said, had Mrs. Ransome ventured to raise the point, but she didn't.

Mrs. Ransome now described the circumstances of the burglary and the extent of their loss, though this made less of an impression on Dusty than it might have done as the diminished state in which the Ransomes were now living—the beanbags, the card table, etc.—

seemed not so much a deprivation to Dusty as it did a style.

Though this was more tidy it was the minimalist look she had opted for in her own flat.

"How near is this to what it was before?" said Dusty.

"Oh, we had a lot more than this," said Mrs. Ransome. "We had everything. It was a normal home."

"I know you must be hurting," said Dusty.

"Hurting what?" asked Mrs. Ransome.

"You. You are hurting."

Mrs. Ransome considered this, her stoicism simply a question of grammar. "Oh. You mean I'm hurt? Well, yes and no. I'm getting used to it, I suppose."

"Don't get used to it too soon," said Dusty. "Give yourself time to grieve. You did weep at the time, I hope?"

"To begin with," said Mrs. Ransome. "But I soon got over it."

"Did Maurice?"

"Maurice?"

"Mr. Ransome."

"Oh . . . no. No. I don't think he did. Well," and it was as if she were sharing a secret, "he's a man, you see."

"No, Rosemary. He's a person. It's a pity that he didn't let himself go at the time. The experts are all more or less agreed that if you don't grieve, keep it all bottled up, you're quite likely at some time in the future to go down with cancer."

"Oh dear," said Mrs. Ransome.

"Of course," said Dusty. "Men do find grieving harder than women. Would it help if I had a word?"

"With Mr. Ransome? No, no," said Mrs. Ransome hastily. "I don't think so. He's very . . . shy."

"Still," said Dusty, "I think I can help you . . . or we can help each other." She leaned over to take Mrs. Ransome's hand but found she couldn't reach it so stroked the beanbag instead.

"They say you feel violated," said Mrs. Ransome.

"Yes. Let it come, Rosemary. Let it come."

"Only I don't particularly. Just mystified."

"Client in denial," Dusty wrote as Mrs. Ransome took away the teacups. Then she added a question mark.

As she was going Dusty suggested that Mrs. Ransome might try to see the whole experience as a learning curve and that one way the curve might go (it could go several ways apparently) was to view the loss of their possessions as a kind of liberation—"the lilies of the field syndrome," as Dusty called it. "Lay-not-up-for-yourself-treasures-on-earth-type thing." This notion having already occurred to Mrs. Ransome she nevertheless didn't immediately take the point because Dusty referred to their belongings as their "gear," a word, which, if it meant anything to Mrs. Ransome, denoted the contents of her handbag—lipstick, compact, etc., none of which she had in fact lost. Though thinking about it afterwards she acknowledged that to lump everything, carpets, curtains, furniture and fittings, all under the term "gear" did make it easier to handle. Still it wasn't a word she contemplated risking on her husband.

Truth to tell (and though she didn't say so to Mrs. Ransome) it was advice Dusty only proffered halfheartedly anyway. The more she saw of the lilies of the field syndrome the less faith she had in it. She'd had one or two clients who'd told her that a hurtful burglary had given them a clue how to live, that from now on they would set less store by material possessions, travel light, etc. Six months later she'd gone back on a follow-up visit to find them more encumbered than ever. Lots of people could give up things, Dusty had decided; what they couldn't do without was shopping for them.

When Mrs. Ransome said to Dusty that she didn't particularly miss her belongings she had been telling the truth. What she did miss—and this was harder to put into words—was not so much the things themselves as her particular paths through them. There was the green bobble hat she had had, for instance, which she never actually wore but would always put on the hall table to remind her that she had switched the immersion heater on in the bathroom. She didn't have the bobble hat now and she didn't have the table to put it on (and that she still had the immersion heater must be regarded as a providence). But with no bobble hat she'd twice left the immersion on all night and once Mr. Ransome had scalded his hand.

He too had had rituals to forgo. He had lost the little curved scissors, for instance, with which he used to cut the hair in his ears—and that was only the beginning of it. While not especially vain he had a little mustache which, if left to itself, had a distasteful tendency to go ginger, a tinge that Mr. Ransome kept in check with the occasional touch of hair dye. This came out of an ancient bottle Mrs. Ransome had tried on her roots years ago and then instantly discarded, but which was still kept at the back of the bathroom cupboard. Locking the bathroom door before applying it to the affected part, Mr.

Ransome had never admitted to what he was doing, with Mrs. Ransome in her turn never admitting that she knew about it anyway. Only now the bathroom cupboard was gone and the bottle with it, so in due course Mr. Ransome's mustache began to take on the telltale orange tinge he found so detestable. Asking her to buy another bottle was one answer but this would be to come clean on the years of clandestine cosmetics. Buying a bottle himself was another. But where? His barber was Polish and his English just about ran to "short back and sides." An understanding chemist perhaps, but all the chemists of Mr. Ransome's acquaintance were anything but understanding, staffed usually by bored little sluts of eighteen unlikely to sympathize with a middle-aged solicitor and his creeping ginger.

Unhappily tracing its progress in Mrs. Ransome's powder compact, kept in the bathroom now as the only mirror in the flat, Mr. Ransome cursed the burglars who had brought such humiliation upon him, and lying on her camp bed Mrs. Ransome reflected that not the least of what they had lost in the burglary were their little marital deceptions.

Mr. Ransome had been told that while the insurance company would not pay for the temporary rental of a CD player (not regarded as an essential) it would sanction the hire of a TV. So one morning Mrs. Ransome went out and chose the most discreet model she could find and it was delivered and fitted that same afternoon. She had never watched daytime television before, feeling she ought to have better things to do. However, when the engineer had gone she found he had left the set switched to some sort of chat show in which an overweight American couple were being questioned by a black lady in a trouser suit about how, as the black lady put it, "they related to one another sexually."

The man, slumped in his seat with his legs wide apart, was describing in as much detail as the woman in the trouser suit would allow what he, as he put it, "asked of his marriage," while the woman, arms folded, knees together but too plump to be prim, was explaining how "without being judgmental, he had never taken the deodorant on board."

"Get a load of that body language," said the lady in the trouser suit, and the audience, mystifyingly to Mrs. Ransome who did not know what body language was, erupted in jeers and laughter.

The things people do for money, thought Mrs. Ransome, and switched it off.

The next afternoon, waking from a doze on her beanbag, she switched on again and found herself watching a similar program with another equally shameless couple and the same hooting, jeering audience, roaming among them with a microphone a different hostess, white this time but as imperturbable as the first and just as oblivious of everybody's bad manners, even, it seemed to Mrs. Ransome, egging them on.

These hostesses (for Mrs. Ransome now began to

generally agreed, needed to talk, and here in front of this jeering throng, hungry for sensation, was the place they had chosen to do it, finally, as the credits rolled, falling hungrily upon one another, mouth glued to mouth while the audience roared its approval and the presenter looked on with a sadder and wiser smile. "Thank you people," she said, and the couple kissed on.

What Mrs. Ransome could never get used to was how unabashed the participants were, how unsheepish, and how none of these people was ever plain shy. Even when there was a program about shyness no one who took part was shy in any sense that Mrs. Ransome understood it; there was no hanging back and no shortage of unblushing participants willing to stand up and boast of their crippling self-consciousness and the absurdities to which overwhelming diffidence and self-effacingness had brought them. No matter how private or intimate the topic under discussion, none of these eager vociferous people had any shame. On the contrary, they seemed to vie with one another in coming up with confessions of behavior that grew ever more ingeniously gross and indelicate; one outrageous admission trumped another, the audience greeting each new revelation with wild whoops and yells, hurling advice at the participants and urging them on to retail new depravities.

There were, it's true, rare occasions when some of the audience gave vent not to glee but to outrage, even seeming for a moment, presented with some particularly egregious confession, to be genuinely shocked; but it was only because the presenter, glancing covertly at the audience behind the speaker's back, had pulled a wry face and so cued their affront. The presenter was an accomplice, Mrs. Ransome thought, and no better than anyone else, even going out of her way to remind participants of yet more inventive and indelicate acts that they had earlier confided to her in the presumed privacy of the dressing room. When she jogged their memories they went through an elaborate pantomime of shame (hiding their heads, covering faces with hands, shaking with seemingly helpless laughter), all this to indicate that they had never expected such secrets to be made public, let alone retailed to the camera.

Still, Mrs. Ransome felt, they were all better than she was. For what none of these whooping, giggling (and often quite obese) creatures seemed in no doubt about was that at the basic level at which these programs were pitched people were all the same. There was no shame and no reserve and to pretend otherwise was to be stuck up and a hypocrite. Mrs. Ransome felt that she was certainly the first and that her husband was probably the second.

The contents of the flat were insured for £50,000. It had originally been much less, but being a solicitor and a careful man besides, Mr. Ransome had seen to it that the premium had kept pace with the cost of living. Accordingly this modest agglomeration of household goods, furniture, fixtures and fittings had gone on over the years gently increasing in value; the stereo and the Magimix, the canteen of cutlery, the EPNS salad servers, the tray cloths and table mats and all the apparatus of that life which the Ransomes had the complete equipment for but had never managed to lead, all this had marched comfortably in step with the index. Durable, sober, unshowy stuff, bought with an eye to use rather than ornament, hardly diminished by breakage or loss, dutifully dusted and polished over the years so that it was scarcely even abraded by wear or tear—all this had gone uneventfully forward until that terrible night when the column had been ambushed and this ordinary, unpretentious little fraternity seemingly wiped out and what Mrs. Ransome modestly called "our things" had vanished forever.

So at any rate the insurance company concluded and in due course a check arrived for the full value plus an unforeseen increment payable in the absence of any previous claims and which served to cover disruption and compensate for distress.

"The extra is for our trauma," said Mrs. Ransome, looking at the check.

"I prefer to call it inconvenience," Mr. Ransome said. "We've been burgled, not knocked down by a bus. Still, the extra will come in handy."

He was already working out a scheme for an improved stereo system plus an update on his CD player combined with high definition digital sound and ultra-refinement of tone, all to be fed through a pair of majestic new speakers in handcrafted mahogany. It would be Mozart as he had never heard him before.

Mrs. Ransome was sitting contentedly in a cheap cane rocking chair she had found a few weeks earlier in a furniture store up the Edgware Road. It was an establishment that, before the burglary, she would never have dreamed of going into, with garish suites, paintings of clowns and, flanking the door, two life-size pottery leopards. A common shop she would have thought it once, as a bit of her still did, but Mr. Anwar had recommended it and sure enough the rocking chair she'd bought there was wonderfully comfortable and, unlike the easy chair in which she used to sit before the burglary, good for her back. Now that the insurance check had come through she planned on getting a matching chair for Mr. Ransome, but in the meantime she had bought a rug to put the chair on, and, sewn with a design of an elephant, it glowed under the light from a brass table lamp bought at the same shop. Sitting with what Mr. Anwar had told her was an Afghan prayer rug round her shoulders she felt in the middle of the bare sitting room floor that she was on a cozy and slightly exotic little island.

For the moment Mr. Ransome's island was not so cozy, just a chair at the card table on which Mrs. Ransome had put the one letter that constituted the day's post. Mr. Ransome picked up the envelope. Smelling curry, he said, "What's for supper?"

"Curry."

Mr. Ransome turned the letter over. It looked like a bill. "What sort of curry?"

"Lamb," said Mrs. Ransome. "With apricots. I've been wondering," she said, "would white be too bold?"

"White what?" said Mr. Ransome, holding the letter up to the light.

"Well," she said hesitantly, "white everything really."

Mr. Ransome did not reply. He was reading the letter.

"You mustn't get too excited," Mr. Ransome said as they were driving toward Aylesbury. "It could be somebody's sense of humor. Another joke."

Actually their mood was quite flat and the countryside was flat too; they had scarcely spoken since they had set off, the letter with Mr. Ransome's penciled directions lying on Mrs. Ransome's lap.

Left at the roundabout, thought Mr. Ransome.

"It's left at the roundabout," Mrs. Ransome said.

He had telephoned the storage firm that morning to have a girl answer. It was called Rapid 'n' Reliant Removals 'n' Storage, those 'n's, Mr. Ransome thought, a foretaste of trouble; nor was he disappointed.

"Hello. Rapid 'n' Reliant Removals 'n' Storage. Christine Thoseby speaking. How may I help you?"

Mr. Ransome asked for Mr. Ralston, who had signed the letter.

"At the present time of speaking Mr. Ralston is in Cardiff. How may I help you?"

"When will he be back?"

"Not until next week. He's on a tour of our repositories. How may I help you?"

Her repeated promises of help notwithstanding, Christine had the practiced lack of interest of someone perpetually painting her nails and when Mr. Ransome explained that the previous day he had received a mysterious invoice for £344.36 re the storage of certain household effects, the property of Mr. and Mrs. Ransome, all Christine said was: "And?" He began to explain the circumstances but at the suggestion that the effects in question might be stolen property Christine came to life.

"May I interject? I think that's very unlikely, quite frankly, I mean, Rapid 'n' Reliant were established in 1977."

Mr. Ransome tried a different tack. "You wouldn't happen to know whether any of these household effects you're holding includes some old stereo equipment?"

"Can't help you there, I'm afraid. But if you have any items in storage with Rapid 'n' Reliant they'll show up on the C47, of which you should have a copy. It's a yellow flimsy."

Mr. Ransome started to explain why he didn't have a flimsy but Christine cut him short.

"I wouldn't know that, would I, because I'm in Newport Pagnell? This is the office. The storage depot is in Aylesbury. You can be anywhere nowadays. It's computers. Actually the person who could help you at Ayles-bury is Martin but I happen to know he's out on a job most of today."

"I wonder whether I ought to go down to Ayles-bury," Mr. Ransome said, "just to see if there's anything there."

Christine was unenthusiastic. "I can't actually stop you," she said, "only they don't have any facilities for visitors. It's not like a kennels," she added inexplicably.

Mr. Ransome having told her the storage firm was in a business park, Mrs. Ransome, who was not familiar with the genre, imagined it situated in a setting agreeably pastoral, a park that was indeed a park and attached to some more or less stately home, now sensitively adapted to modern requirements; the estate dotted with work-shops possibly; offices nestling discreetly in trees. At the hub of this center of enterprise she pictured a country house where tall women with folders strode along ter-races, typists busied themselves in gilded saloons beneath painted ceilings, a vision that, had she thought to trace it back, she would have found to have derived from those war films where French châteaux taken over by the German High Command bustle with new life on the eve of D-Day.

It was as well she didn't share these romantic expectations with Mr. Ransome who, the secretary of several companies and thus acquainted with the reality, would have given them short shrift.

It was only when she found herself being driven round a bleak treeless ring road lined with small factories and surrounded by concrete and rough grass that Mrs. Ransome began to revise her expectations.

"It doesn't look very countrified," Mrs. Ransome said.

"Why should it?" said Mr. Ransome, about to turn in at some un-Palladian metal gates.

"This is it," said Mrs. Ransome, looking at the letter.

The gates were set in a seven-foot-high fence topped

with an oblique pelmet of barbed wire so that the place looked less like a park than a prison. Fixed to an empty pillbox was a metal diagram, painted in yellow and blue, showing the whereabouts of the various firms on the estate. Mr. Ransome got out to look for Unit 14.

"You are here," said an arrow, only someone had inserted at the tip of the arrow a pair of crudely drawn buttocks.

Unit 14 appeared to be a few hundred yards inside the perimeter, just about where, had the buttocks been drawn to scale, the navel might have been. Mr. Ransome got back in the car and drove slowly on in the gathering dusk until he came to a broad low hangarlike building with double sliding doors, painted red and bare of all identification except for a warning that guard dogs patrolled. There were no other cars and no sign of anybody about.

Mr. Ransome pulled at the sliding door, not expecting to find it open. Nor was it.

"It's locked," said Mrs. Ransome.

"You don't say," Mr. Ransome muttered under his breath, and struck out round the side of the building, followed more slowly by Mrs. Ransome, picking her way uncertainly over the rubble and clinkers and patches of scrubby grass. Mr. Ransome felt his shoe skid on something.

"Mind the dog dirt," said Mrs. Ransome. "It's all over this grass." Steps led down to a basement door. Mr. Ransome tried this too. It was also locked, a boiler room possibly.

"That looks like a boiler room," said Mrs. Ransome.

He scraped his shoe on the step.

"You'd think they'd make them set an example," Mrs. Ransome said.

"Who?" said Mr. Ransome, slurring his polluted shoe over some thin grass.

"The guard dogs."

They had almost completed a circuit of the hangar

when they came on a small frosted window where there was a dim light. It was open an inch or two at the top and was obviously a lavatory, and faintly through the glass Mrs. Ransome could see standing on the window ledge the blurred shape of a toilet roll. It was doubtless a co-incidence that it was blue, and forget-me-not blue at that, a shade Mrs. Ransome always favored in her own toilet rolls and which was not always easy to find. She pressed her face to the glass in order to see it more clearly and then saw something else.

"Look, dear," Mrs. Ransome said. But Mr. Ransome wasn't looking. He was listening.

"Shut up," he said. He could hear Mozart.

And floating through the crack of the lavatory window came the full, dark, sumptuous and utterly unmis-takable tones of Dame Kiri Te Kanawa.

"Per pietà, ben mio," she was singing, *"perdona all'error d'un amante."*

And out it drifted into the damp dusk, rising over

69

Rapid 'n' Reliant at Unit 14 and Croda Adhesives at Unit 16 and Lansyl Sealant Applicators PLC at Unit 20 (Units 17–19 currently under offer).

"O Dio," sang Dame Kiri. *"O Dio."*

And the perimeter road heard it and the sheathed and stunted saplings planted there and the dirty dribble of a stream that straggled through a concrete culvert to the lumpy field beyond, where a shabby horse contemplated two barrels and a pole.

Galvanized by the sound of the antipodean songstress Mr. Ransome clambered up the fall pipe and knelt painfully on the windowsill. Clinging to the pipe with one hand he prized open the window an inch or two further and forced his head in as far as it would go, almost slipping off the sill in the process.

"Careful," said Mrs. Ransome.

Mr. Ransome began to shout. "Hello. Hello?"

Mozart stopped and somewhere a bus went by.

In the silence Mr. Ransome shouted again, this time almost joyfully. "Hello!"

Instantly there was bedlam. Dogs burst out barking, a siren went off and Mr. and Mrs. Ransome were trapped and dazzled by half a dozen security lights focused tightly on their shrinking forms. Petrified, Mr. Ransome clung desperately to the lavatory window while Mrs. Ransome plastered herself as closely as she could against the wall, one hand creeping (she hoped unobtrusively) up the windowsill to seek the comfort of Mr. Ransome's knee.

Then, as suddenly as it had begun, the commotion stopped; the lights went out, the siren trailed off and the barking of the dogs modulated to an occasional growl. Trembling on the sill Mr. Ransome heard a door pushed back and unhurried steps walking across the forecourt.

"Sorry about that, people," said a male voice. "Burglars, I'm afraid, measures for the detection and discouragement of."

Mrs. Ransome peered into the darkness but still half-blinded by the lights could see nothing. Mr. Ransome slithered down the fall pipe to stand beside her and she took his hand.

"This way chaps and chapesses. Over here."

Mr. and Mrs. Ransome stumbled across the last of the grass onto the concrete where silhouetted against the open door stood a young man.

Dazed, they followed him into the hangar and in the light they made a sorry-looking pair. Mrs. Ransome was limping because one of her heels had broken and she had laddered both her stockings. Mr. Ransome had torn the knee of his trousers; there was shit on his shoes, and across his forehead where he had pressed his face into the window was a long black smudge.

The young man smiled and put out his hand. "Maurice. Rosemary. Hi! I'm Martin."

It was a pleasant open face and though he did have
one of those little beards Mrs. Ransome thought made
them all look like poisoners, for a warehouseman one
way and another he looked quite classy. True he was
wearing the kind of cap that had once been the distinctive headgear of American golfers but now seemed
of general application, and a little squirt of hair with
a rubber band around it was coming out of the back,
and, again like them all nowadays, his shirttail was
out; still, what gave him a certain air in Mrs. Ransome's
eyes was his smart maroon cardigan. It was not unlike one she had picked out for Mr. Ransome at a
Simpson's sale the year before. Loosely knotted around
his neck was a yellow silk scarf with horses' heads
on it. Mrs. Ransome had bought Mr. Ransome one of
those too, though he had worn it only once as he decided it made him look like a cad. This boy didn't look
like a cad; he looked dashing and she thought that if
they ever got their belongings back she'd root the scarf

sofa, their high-backed chairs, the reproduction walnut-veneered coffee table with the scalloped edges and cabriole legs and on it the latest number of the *Gramophone*. Here was Mrs. Ransome's embroidery, lying on the end of the sofa where she had put it down before going to change at a quarter to six on that never-to-be-forgotten evening. There on the nest of tables was the glass from which Mr. Ransome had had a little drop of something to see him through the first act of *Così*, still (Mrs. Ransome touched the rim of the glass with her finger) slightly sticky.

On the mantelpiece the carriage clock, presented to Mr. Ransome to mark his twenty-five years with the firm of Selvey, Ransome, Steele and Co., struck six, though Mrs. Ransome was not sure if it was six then or six now. The lights were on, just as they had left them.

"A waste of electricity, I know," Mr. Ransome was wont to say, "but at least it deters the casual thief," and on the hall table was the evening paper left there by Mr.

Ransome for Mrs. Ransome, who generally read it with her morning coffee the following day.

Other than a cardboard plate with some cold half-eaten curry which Martin neatly heeled under the sofa, mouthing "Sorry," everything, every little thing, was exactly as it should be; they might have been at home in their flat in Naseby Mansions, St. John's Wood, and not in a hangar on an industrial estate on the outskirts of nowhere.

Gone was the feeling of foreboding with which Mrs. Ransome had set out that afternoon; now there was only joy as she wandered round the room, occasionally picking up some cherished object with a smile and an "Oh!" of reacquaintance, sometimes holding it up for her husband to see. For his part Mr. Ransome was almost moved, particularly when he spotted his old CD player, his trusty old CD player as he was inclined to think of it now, not quite up to the mark, it's true, the venerable old thing, but still honest and old-fashioned; yes, it was good to see it again and he gave Mrs. Ransome a brief blast of *Così*.

Watching this reunion with a smile almost of pride, Martin said, "Everything in order? I tried to keep it all just as it was."

"Oh yes," said Mrs. Ransome, "it's perfect."

"Astonishing," said her husband.

Mrs. Ransome remembered something. "I'd put a casserole in the oven."

"Yes," said Martin, "I enjoyed that."

"It wasn't dry?" said Mrs. Ransome.

"Only a touch," said Martin, following them into the bedroom. "It would perhaps have been better at Gas Mark 3."

Mrs. Ransome nodded and noticed on the dressing table the piece of kitchen paper (she remembered how they had run out of Kleenex) with which she had blotted her lipstick three months before.

"Kitchen," said Martin as if they might not know

the way, though it was exactly where it should have been, and exactly how too, except that the casserole dish, now empty, stood washed and waiting on the draining board.

"I wasn't sure where that went," said Martin apologetically.

"That's all right," said Mrs. Ransome. "It lives in here." She opened the cupboard by the sink and popped the dish away.

"That was my guess," said Martin, "though I didn't like to risk it." He laughed and Mrs. Ransome laughed too.

Mr. Ransome scowled. The young man was civil enough, if overfamiliar, but it all seemed a bit too relaxed. A crime had been committed after all, and not a petty one either; this was stolen property; what was it doing here?

Mr. Ransome thought it was time to take charge of the situation.

"Tea?" said Martin.

"No thank you," said Mr. Ransome.

"Yes please," said his wife.

"Then," said Martin, "we need to talk."

Mrs. Ransome had never heard the phrase used in real life as it were and she looked at this young man with newfound recognition: she knew where he was coming from. So did Mr. Ransome.

"Yes, indeed," said Mr. Ransome, decisively, sitting down at the kitchen table and meaning to kick off by asking this altogether-too-pleased-with-himself young man what this was all about.

"Perhaps," said Martin, giving Mrs. Ransome her tea, "perhaps you would like to tell me what this is all about. I mean with all due respect, as they say."

This was too much for Mr. Ransome.

"Perhaps," he exploded, "and with all due respect, you'd like to tell me why it is you're wearing my cardigan."

"You never wore it much," said Mrs. Ransome placidly. "Lovely tea."

"That isn't the point, Rosemary." Mr. Ransome seldom used her Christian name except as a form of blunt instrument. "And that's my silk scarf."

"You never wore that at all. You said it made you look like a cad."

"That's why I like it," said Martin, happily, "the cad factor. However all good things come to an end, as they say." And unhurriedly (and quite unrepentantly, thought Mr. Ransome) he took off the cardigan, unknotted the scarf and laid them both on the table.

Pruned of these sheltering encumbrances, Martin's T-shirt, the message of which had hitherto only been hinted at, now fearlessly proclaimed itself, "Got a stiffy? Wear a Jiffy!" and in brackets "drawing on back." As Mr. Ransome eased forward in his chair in order to shield his wife from the offending illustration, Mrs. Ransome slightly eased back.

"Actually," said Martin, "we've worn one or two of your things. I started off with your brown overcoat which I just tried on originally as a bit of a joke."

"A joke?" said Mr. Ransome, the humorous qualities of that particular garment never having occurred to him.

"Yes. Only now I've grown quite fond of it. It's great."

"But it must be too big for you," said Mrs. Ransome.

"I know. That's why it's so great. And you've got tons of scarves. Cleo thinks you've got really good taste."

"Cleo?" said Mrs. Ransome.

"My partner."

Then, catching sight of Mr. Ransome by now pop-eyed with fury, Martin shrugged. "After all, it was you who gave us the green light." He went into the sitting room and came back with a folder, which he laid on the kitchen table.

"Just tell me," said Mr. Ransome with terrible calmness, "why it is our things are here."

So Martin explained. Except it wasn't really an explanation and when he'd finished they weren't much further on.

He had come in to work one morning about three months ago ("February 15," Mrs. Ransome supplied helpfully) and unlocking the doors had found their flat set out just as it had been in Naseby Mansions and just as they saw it now—carpets down, lights on, warm, a smell of cooking from the kitchen.

"I mean," said Martin happily, *"home."*

"But surely," Mr. Ransome said, "you must have realized that this was, to say the least, unusual?"

"Very unusual," said Martin. Normally, he said, home contents were containered, crated and sealed, and the container parked in the back lot until required. "We store loads of furniture, but I might go for six months and never see an armchair."

"But why were they all dumped here?" said Mrs. Ransome.

"Dumped?" said Martin. "You call this dumped? It's beautiful, it's a poem."

"Why?" said Mr. Ransome.

"Well, when I came in that morning, there was an envelope on the hall table. . . ."

"That's where I put the letters normally," said Mrs. Ransome.

". . . an envelope," said Martin, "containing £3000 in cash to cover storage costs for two months, well clear of our normal charges I can tell you. And," said Martin, taking a card out of the folder, "there was this."

It was a sheet torn from the *Delia Smith Cookery Calendar* with a recipe for the hotpot that Mrs. Ransome had made that afternoon and which she had left in the oven. On the back of it was written: "Leave exactly as it is," and then in brackets, "but feel free to use." This was underlined.

"So, where your overcoat was concerned and the scarves et cetera, I felt," said Martin, searching for the right word, "I felt that that was my *imprimatur.*" (He had been briefly at the University of Warwick.)

"But anybody could have written that," Mr. Ransome said.

"And leave £3000 in cash with it?" said Martin. "No fear. Only I did check. Newport Pagnell knew nothing about it. Cardiff. Leeds. I had it run through the computer and they drew a complete blank. So I thought, Well, Martin, the stuff's here. For the time being it's paid for, so why not just make yourself at home? So I did. I could have done with the choice of CDs being a bit more eclectic, though. My guess is you're a Mozart fan?"

"I still think," said Mr. Ransome testily, "you might have made more inquiries before making so free with our belongings."

"It's not usual, I agree," said Martin. "Only why should I? I'd no reason to . . . smell a rat?"

Mr. Ransome took in (and was irritated by) these occasional notes of inappropriate interrogation with which Martin (and the young generally) seemed often to end a sentence. He had heard it in the mouth of the office boy without realizing it had got as far as Aylesbury ("And where are you going now, Foster?" "For my lunch?"). It seemed insolent, though it was hard to say why and it invariably put Mr. Ransome in a bad temper (which was why Foster did it).

Martin on the other hand seemed unconscious of the irritation he was causing, his serenity so impervious Mr. Ransome put it down to drugs. Now he sat happily at the kitchen table, and while Mr. Ransome fussed around the flat on the lookout for evidence of damage or dilapidation or even undue wear and tear, Martin chatted comfortably to Rosemary, as he called her.

"He just needs to lighten up a bit," said Martin as Mr. Ransome banged about in the cupboards.

Mrs. Ransome wasn't sure if "lighten up" was the

85

same as "brighten up" but catching his drift smiled and nodded.

"It's been like playing houses," said Martin. "Cleo and I live over a dry cleaners normally."

Mrs. Ransome thought Cleo might be black but she didn't like to ask.

"Actually," said Martin, dropping his voice because Mr. Ransome was in the pantry cupboard counting the bottles of wine in the rack, "actually it's perked things up between us two. Change of scene, you know what they say."

Mrs. Ransome nodded knowledgeably; it was a topic frequently touched on in the afternoon programs.

"Good bed," whispered Martin. "The mattress gives you lots of—what's the word?—purchase." Martin gave a little thrust with his hips. "Know what I mean, Rose-mary?" He winked.

"It's orthopedic," Mrs. Ransome said hastily. "Mr. Ransome has a bad back."

"I'd probably have one too if I'd lived here much longer." Martin patted her hand. "Only joking."

"What I don't understand," said Mr. Ransome, coming into the kitchen while Martin still had his hand over his wife's (Mr. Ransome didn't understand that either), "what I don't understand is how whoever it was that transported our things here could remember so exactly where everything went."

"Trouble ye no more," said Martin, and he went out into the hall and brought back a photograph album. It was a present Mr. Ransome had bought Mrs. Ransome when he was urging her to find a hobby. He had also bought her a camera which she had never managed to fathom so that the camera never got used, nor did the album. Except that now it was full of photographs.

"The Polaroid camera," Martin said, "the blessings thereof."

There were a dozen or so photographs for every room in the flat on the night in question; general views of the room, corners of the room, a close-up of the mantelpiece, another of the desktop, every room and every surface recorded in conscientious detail, much as if, had the flat been the setting for a film, the continuity assistant would have recorded them.

"And our name and address?" Mr. Ransome said.

"Simple," said Martin. "Open . . ."

"Any drawer," said he and Mrs. Ransome together.

"All these photographs," Mrs. Ransome said. "Whoever they are, they must have no end of money. Don't they make it look nice."

"It is nice," said Martin. "We're going to miss it."

"It's not only that all our things are in the right place," Mr. Ransome said. "The rooms are in the right place too."

"Screens," said Martin. "They must have brought screens with them."

"There's no ceiling," said Mr. Ransome triumphantly. "They didn't manage that."

"They managed the chandelier," said his wife. And so they had, suspending it from a handy beam.

"Well, I don't think we need to prolong this stage of the proceedings any longer than we have to," said Mr. Ransome. "I'll contact my insurance company and tell them our belongings have been found. They will then doubtless contact you over their collection and return. There doesn't seem to be anything missing but at this stage one can't be sure."

"Oh, there's nothing missing," said Martin. "One or two After Eights perhaps, but I can easily replenish those."

"No, no," said Mrs. Ransome, "that won't be necessary. They're"—and she smiled—"they're on the house."

Mr. Ransome frowned and when Martin went off to find the various pro-formas he whispered to Mrs. Ransome that they would have to have everything cleaned.

"I don't like to think what's been going on. There was a bit of kitchen paper on your dressing table with what was almost certainly blood. And I've a feeling they may have been sleeping in our bed."

"We'll exchange flimsies," said Martin. "One flimsy for you. One flimsy for me. Your effects. Do you say 'effects' when a person's still around? Or is it just when they're dead?"

"Dead," said Mr. Ransome authoritatively. "In this case it's property."

"Effects," said Martin. "Good word."

Standing on the forecourt as they were going Martin kissed Mrs. Ransome on both cheeks. He was about the age their son would have been, Mrs. Ransome thought, had they had a son.

"I feel like I'm one of the family," he said.

Yes, thought Mr. Ransome; if they'd had a son this is what it would have been like. Irritating, perplexing. Feeling got at. They wouldn't have been able to call their lives their own.

Mr. Ransome managed to shake hands.

"All's well that ends well," said Martin, and patted his shoulder. "Take care."

"How do we know he wasn't in on it?" said Mr. Ransome in the car.

"He doesn't look the type," said Mrs. Ransome.

"Oh? What type is that? Have you ever come across a case like this before? Have you ever heard of it? What type does it take, that's what I'd like to know."

"We're going a little fast," said Mrs. Ransome.

"I shall have to inform the police, of course," Mr. Ransome said.

"They weren't interested before so they'll be even less interested now."

"Who are you?"

"Beg pardon?"

"I'm the solicitor. Who are you? Are you the expert?"

They drove in silence for a while.

"Of course, I shall want some compensation. The

distress. The agony of mind. The inconvenience. They're all quantifiable, and must be taken into account in the final settlement."

He was already writing the letter in his head.

In due course, the contents of the flat came back to Naseby Mansions, a card pinned to one of the crates saying, "Feel Free to Use. Martin." And, in brackets, "Joke." Mr. Ransome insisted that everything must be put back just as it had been before, which might have proved difficult had it not been for the aide-mémoire in the form of Mrs. Ransome's photograph album. Even so the gang who returned the furniture were less meticulous than the burglars who had removed it, besides being much slower. Still, the flat having been decorated throughout and the covers washed, hoovered or dry-cleaned, the place gradually came to look much as it had done before and life returned to what Mrs. Ransome used to think of as normal but didn't now, quite.

Quite early on in the proceedings, and while Mr.

Ransome was at the office, Mrs. Ransome tried out her cane rocking chair and rug in the now much less spartan conditions of the lounge, but though the chair was as comfortable as ever the ensemble didn't look right and made her feel she was sitting in a department store. So she relegated the chair to the spare room where from time to time she visited it and sat reviewing her life. But no, it was not the same and eventually she put the chair out for the caretaker who incorporated it into his scheme of things in the room behind the boiler, where he was now trying to discover the books of Jane Austen.

Mr. Ransome fared better than his wife, for although he had had to reimburse the insurance company over their original check he was able to claim that having already ordered some new speakers (he hadn't) this should be taken into account and allowance made, which it duly was, thus enabling him to invest in some genuinely state-of-the-art equipment.

From time to time over the next few months traces

of Martin and Cleo's brief occupation would surface—
a contraceptive packet (empty) that had been thrust
under the mattress, a handkerchief down the side of the
settee and, in one of the mantelpiece ornaments, a lump
of hard brown material wrapped in silver paper. Tenta-
tively Mrs. Ransome sniffed it, then donned her Mari-
gold gloves and put it down the lavatory, assuming that
was where it belonged, though it was only after several
goes that it was reluctantly flushed, Mrs. Ransome sitting meanwhile on the side of the bath, waiting for the
cistern to refill, and wondering how it came to be on the
mantelpiece in the first place. A joke possibly, though
not one she shared with Mr. Ransome.

Strange hairs were another item that put in regular
appearances, long fair ones which were obviously Martin's, darker crinklier ones she supposed must be Cleo's.
The incidence of these hairs wasn't split evenly between
Mr. and Mrs. Ransome's respective wardrobes; indeed,

since Mr. Ransome didn't complain about them, she presumed he never found any, as he would certainly have let her know if he had.

She, on the other hand, found them everywhere— among her dresses, her coats, her underwear, his hairs as well as hers, and little ones as well as long ones, so that she was left puzzling over what it was they could have been up to that wasn't constrained by the normal boundaries of gender and propriety. Had Martin worn her knickers on his head, she wondered (in one pair there were three hairs); had the elastic on her brassiere always been as loose as it was now (two hairs there, one fair, one dark)?

Still, sitting opposite Mr. Ransome in his earphones of an evening, she could contemplate with equanimity, and even a small thrill, that she had shared her under-clothes with a third party. Or two third parties possibly. "You don't mean a third party," Mr. Ransome would have said, but this was another argument for keeping quiet.

There was one reminder of the recent past, though, that they were forced to share, if only by accident. They had had their supper one Saturday evening after which Mr. Ransome was planning to record a live broadcast of *Il Seraglio* on Radio 3. Mrs. Ransome, reflecting that there was never anything on TV worth watching on a Saturday night, had settled down to read a novel about some lackluster infidelities in a Cotswold setting while Mr. Ransome prepared to record. He had put in a tape that he thought was blank but checking it on the machine was startled to find that it began with a peal of helpless laughter. Mrs. Ransome looked up. Mr. Ransome listened long enough to detect that there were two people laughing, a man and a woman, and since they showed no sign of stopping was about to switch it off when Mrs. Ransome said, "No, Maurice. Leave it. This might be a clue."

So they listened in silence as the laughter went on, almost uninterrupted, until after three or four minutes it began to slacken and break up and whoever it was who was still laughing was left panting and breathless, this breathlessness gradually modulating into another sound, the second subject as it were, a groan and then a cry leading to a rhythmic pumping as stern and as purposeful as the other had been silly and lighthearted. At one point the microphone was moved closer to catch a sound that was so moist and wet it hardly seemed human.

"It sounds," said Mrs. Ransome, "like custard boiling," though she knew that it wasn't. Making custard must seldom be so effortful as this seemed to be, nor is the custard urged on with affirmative yells, nor do the cooks cry out when, in due course, the custard starts to boil over.

"I don't think we want to listen to this, do we?" Mr. Ransome said and switched over to Radio 3, where they came in on the reverent hush that preceded the arrival of Claudio Abbado.

Later when they were in bed Mrs. Ransome said, "I suppose we'd better return that tape?"

"What for?" said Mr. Ransome. "The tape is mine. In any case, we can't. It's wiped. I recorded over it."

This was a lie. Mr. Ransome had wanted to record over it, it's true, but felt that whenever he listened to the music he would remember what lay underneath and this would put paid to any possible sublimity. So he had put the tape in the kitchen bin. Then, thinking about it as Mrs. Ransome was in the bathroom brushing her teeth, he went and delved among the potato peelings and old tea bags, and, picking off a tomato skin that had stuck to it, he hid the cassette in the bookcase behind a copy of *Salmon on Torts*, a hidey-hole where he also kept a cache of photographs of some suburban sexual acts, the legacy of a messy divorce case in Epsom that he had conducted a few years before. The bookcase had, of course, gone to Aylesbury along with everything else but had been returned intact, the hiding place seemingly undetected by Martin.

Actually it had not been undetected at all: the photographs had been what he and Cleo had been laughing about on the tape in the first place.

Not a secret from Martin, nor were the snaps a secret from Mrs. Ransome who, idly looking at the bookcase one afternoon and wondering what to cook for supper, had seen the title *Salmon on Torts* and thought it had a vaguely culinary sound to it. She had put the photographs back undisturbed but every few months or so would check to see that they were still there. When they were she felt somehow reassured.

So sometimes now when Mr. Ransome sat in his chair with his earphones on listening to *The Magic Flute* it was not *The Magic Flute* he was listening to at all. Gazing abstractedly at his reading wife his ears were full of Martin and Cleo moaning and crying and taking it out on one another again and again and again. No matter how often he listened to the tape Mr. Ransome never ceased to be amazed by it; that two human beings could give themselves up so utterly and unreservedly to one another and to the moment was beyond his comprehension; it seemed to him miraculous.

Listening to the tape so often he became every bit as familiar with it as with something by Mozart. He came to recognize Martin's long intake of breath as marking the end of a mysterious bridging passage (Cleo was actually on hands and knees, Martin behind her) when the languorous andante (little mewings from the girl) accelerated into the percussive allegro assai (hoarse cries from them both) which in its turn gave way to an even more frantic coda, a sudden rallentando ("No, no, not yet," she was crying, then "Yes, yes, yes") followed by panting, sighing, silence and finally sleep. Not an imaginative man, Mr. Ransome nevertheless found himself thinking that if one built up a library of such tapes it would be possible to bestow on them the sexual equivalent of Köchel numbers, even trace the development of some sort of style in sexual intercourse, with early, middle and late periods, the whole apparatus of Mozartean musicology adapted to these new and thwacking rhythms.

Such were Mr. Ransome's thoughts as he sat across from his wife, who was having another stab at Barbara Pym. She knew he wasn't listening to Mozart though there were few obvious signs and nothing so vulgar as a bulge in his trousers. No, there was just a look of strain on Mr. Ransome's face, which was the very opposite of the look he had when he was listening to his favorite composer; an intensity of attention and a sense that, were he to listen hard enough, he might hear something on the tape he had previously missed.

Mrs. Ransome would listen to the tape herself from time to time but lacking the convenient camouflage of Mozart she confined her listening experiences to the afternoons. Getting out her folding household steps she would pull down *Salmon on Torts* then reach in behind it for the tape (the photographs seemed as silly and laughable to her as they had to Martin and Cleo). Then, having poured herself a small sherry, she would settle down to listen to them making love, marveling still after at least a dozen hearings at the length and persistence of the process and its violent and indecorous outcome. Afterwards she would go and lie on the bed, reflecting that this was the same bed on which it had all happened and think again about it happening.

These discreet (and discrete) epiphanies apart, life after they had recovered their possessions went on much the same as it had before they lost them. Sometimes, though, lying there on the bed or waiting to get up in the morning, Mrs. Ransome would get depressed, feeling she had missed the bus; though what bus it was or where it was headed she would have found it hard to say. Prior to the visit to Aylesbury and the return of their things, she had, she thought, persuaded herself that the

burglary had been an opportunity, with each day bringing its crop of small adventures—a visit from Dusty, a
walk down to Mr. Anwar's, a trip up the Edgware Road.
Now, re-ensconced among her possessions, Mrs. Ransome feared that her diversions were at an end; life had
returned to normal but it was a normal she no longer
relished or was contented with.

The afternoons particularly were dull and full of regret. It's true she continued to watch the television, no
longer so surprised at what people got up to as she once
had been but even (as with Martin and Cleo) mildly en-
vious. She grew so accustomed to the forms of television
discourse that she occasionally let slip a telltale phrase
herself, remarking once, for instance, that there had
been a bit of hassle on the 74 bus.

"Hassle?" said Mr. Ransome. "Where did you pick
up that expression?"

"Why?" said Mrs. Ransome innocently. "Isn't it a
proper word?"

"Not in my vocabulary."

It occurred to Mrs. Ransome that this was the time for counseling; previously an option it had now become a necessity so she tried to reach Dusty via her Help-line.

"I'm sorry but Ms. Briscoe is not available to take your call," said a recorded voice, which was immediately interrupted by a real presence.

"Hello. Mandy speaking. How may I help you?"

Mrs. Ransome explained that she needed to talk to somebody about the sudden return of all the stolen property. "I have complicated feelings about it," said Mrs. Ransome and tried to explain.

Mandy was doubtful. "It might come under post-traumatic stress syndrome," she said, "only I wouldn't bank on it. They're clamping down on that now we're coming to the end of this year's financial year, and anyway it's meant for rape and murder and whatnot, whereas we've had people ringing up who've just had a bad time at the dentist's. You don't feel the furniture's dirty, do you?"

"No," said Mrs. Ransome. "We've had everything cleaned anyway."

"Well, if you've kept the receipts I could ring Bickerton Road and get them to give you something back."

"Never mind," said Mrs. Ransome. "I expect I shall cope."

"Well, it's what we all have to do in the end, isn't it?" said Mandy.

"What's that?" said Mrs. Ransome.

"Cope, dear. After all, that's the name of the game. And the way you've described it," Mandy said, "it seems a very *caring* burglary."

Mandy was right, though it was the caringness that was the problem. Had this been a burglary in the ordinary way it would have been easier to get over. Even the comprehensive removal of everything they had in the world was something Mrs. Ransome could have adjusted to, been "positive" about, even enjoyed. But it was the wholesale disappearance coupled with the meticulous reconstruction and return that rankled. Who would want to rob them to that degree and having robbed them would choose to make such immaculate reparations? It seemed to Mrs. Ransome that she had been robbed twice over, by the loss, first, of her possessions, then of the chance to transcend that loss. It was not fair, nor did it make sense; she thought perhaps this was what they meant when they talked about "losing the plot."

People seldom wrote to the Ransomes. They had the occasional card from Canada where Mr. Ransome had some relatives of his mother who dutifully kept up the connection; Mrs. Ransome would write back, her card as flavorless as theirs, the message from Canada little more than "Hello. We are still here," and her reply, "Yes, and so are we." Generally, though, the post consisted of bills and business communications, and picking them up from the box downstairs in the lobby Mrs. Ransome scarcely bothered to look them through, putting them unsifted on the hall table where Mr. Ransome would deal with them before he had his supper. On this particular morning she'd just completed this ritual when she noticed that the letter on top was from South America, and that it was not addressed to Mr. M. Ransome but to a Mr. M. Hanson. This had happened once before, Mr. Ransome putting the misdirected letter in the caretaker's box with a note asking him or the post-man to be more careful in future.

Less tolerant of her husband's fussing than she once had been, Mrs. Ransome didn't want this performance again so she put the letter on one side so that after her lunch she could go up to the eighth floor, find Mr. Hanson's door and slip it underneath. At least it would be an outing.

It was several years since she had been up to the top of the Mansions. There had been some alterations, she knew, as Mr. Ransome had had to write a letter of complaint to the landlords about the noise of the workmen and the dirt in the lift; but, as tenants came and went, someone was always having something done somewhere and Mrs. Ransome came to take renovation as a fact of life. Still, venturing out of the lift she was surprised how airy it all was now; it might have been a modern building, so light and unshadowed and spacious was the landing. Unlike their dark and battered mahogany, this woodwork had been stripped and bleached, and whereas their hallway was covered in stained and pockmarked orange floor covering, this had a thick smoky-blue fitted carpet that lapped the walls and muffled every sound. Above was a high octagonal skylight and beneath it an octagonal sofa to match. It looked less like the hallway of a block of mansion flats than a hotel or one of the new hospitals. Nor was it simply the decoration that had changed. Mrs. Ransome remembered there being several flats but now there seemed to be only one, no trace of the other doors remaining. She looked for a name on this one door just to be sure but there was no name and no letter box. She bent down intending to slip the letter from South America underneath but the carpet was so thick that this was difficult and it wouldn't go. Above Mrs. Ransome's head and unseen by her, a security camera, which she had taken for a light fitting, moved around like some clumsy reptile in a series of silent jerks until it had her in frame. She was trying to press the pile of the carpet down when there was a faint buzz and the door swung silently open.

"Come in," said a disembodied voice and holding up the letter as if it were an invitation Mrs. Ransome went in.

There was no one in the hall and she waited uncertainly, smiling helpfully in case someone was watching. The hall was identical in shape to theirs but twice the size and done up like the lobby in the same blond wood and faintly stippled walls. They must have knocked through, she thought, taken in the flat next door, taken

in all the flats probably, the whole of the top floor one
flat.

"I brought a letter," she said, more loudly than if
there had been someone there. "It came by mistake."

There was no sound.

"I think it's from South America. Peru. That is if the
name's Hanson. Anyway," she said desperately, "I'll just
put it down then go."

She was about to put the letter down on a cube of
transparent Perspex which she took to be a table when
she heard behind her an exhausted sigh and turned to
find that the door had closed. But as the door behind
her closed so, with a mild intake of breath, the door in
front of her opened, and through it she saw another
doorway, this one with a bar across the top, and sus-
pended from the bar a young man.

He was pulling himself up to the bar seemingly
without much effort, and saying his score out loud. He
was wearing gray track suit bottoms and earphones and

that was all. He had reached eleven. Mrs. Ransome waited, still holding up the letter and not quite sure where to look. It was a long time since she had been so close to someone so young and so naked, the trousers slipping down low over his hips so that she could see the thin line of blond hair climbing the flat belly to his navel. He was tiring now and the last two pull-ups, nineteen and twenty, cost him great effort and after he had almost shouted "Twenty" he stood there panting, one hand still grasping the bar, the earphones low round his neck. There was a faint graze of hair under his arms and some just beginning on his chest and like Martin he had the same squirt of hair at the back though his was longer and twisted into a knot.

Mrs. Ransome thought she had never seen anyone so beautiful in all her life.

"I brought a letter," she began again. "It came by mistake."

She held it out to him but he made no move to take it, so she looked around for somewhere to put it down.

There was a long refectory table down the middle of the room and by the wall a sofa that was nearly as long, but these were the only objects in the room that Mrs. Ransome would have called proper furniture. There were some brightly colored plastic cubes scattered about which she supposed might serve as occasional tables, or possibly stools. There was a tall steel pyramid with vents that seemed to be a standard lamp. There was an old-fashioned pram with white-walled tires and huge curved springs. On one wall was a dray horse collar and on another a cavalier's hat and next to it a huge blown-up photograph of Lana Turner.

"She was a film star," the young man said. "It's an original."

"Yes, I remember," Mrs. Ransome said.

"Why, did you know her?"

"Oh no," Mrs. Ransome said. "Anyway, she was American."

The floor was covered in a thick white carpet which she imagined would show every mark though there were no marks that she could see. Still, it didn't seem to Mrs. Ransome to add up, this room, and with one of the walls glass, giving out onto a terrace, it felt less like a room than an unfinished window display in a department store, a bolt of tweed flung casually across the table what it needed somehow to make sense.

He saw her looking.

"It's been in magazines," he said. "Sit down," and he took the letter from her.

He sat at one end of the sofa and she sat at the other. He put his feet up and if she had put her feet up too there would still have been plenty of room between them. He looked at the letter, turning it over once or twice without opening it.

"It's from Peru," Mrs. Ransome said.

"Yes," he said, "thanks," and tore it in two.

"It might be important," said Mrs. Ransome.

"It's always important," said the young man, and dropped the pieces on the carpet.

Mrs. Ransome looked at his feet. Like every bit of him that she could see they were perfect, the toes not bent up and useless like her own, or Mr. Ransome's. These were long, square-cut and even expressive; they looked as if at a pinch they could deputize for the hands and even play a musical instrument.

"I've never seen you in the lift," she said.

"I have a key. Then it doesn't have to stop at the other floors." He smiled. "It's handy."

"Not for us," said Mrs. Ransome.

"That's true," and he laughed, unoffended. "Anyway, I pay extra."

"I didn't know you could do that," said Mrs. Ransome.

"You can't," he said.

Mrs. Ransome had an idea he was a singer, but felt that if she asked he might cease to treat her as an equal. She also wondered if he was on drugs. Silence certainly didn't seem to bother him and he lay back at his end of the sofa, smiling and completely at ease.

"I should go," said Mrs. Ransome.

"Why?"

He felt in his armpit then waved an arm at the room.

"This is all her."

"Who?"

He indicated the torn-up letter. "She did the place up. She's an interior decorator. Or was. She now ranches in Peru."

"Cattle?" said Mrs. Ransome.

"Horses."

"Oh," said Mrs. Ransome. "That's nice. There can't be too many people who've done that."

"Done what?"

"Been an interior decorator then . . . then . . . looked after horses."

He considered this. "No. Though she was like that. You know, sporadic." He surveyed the room. "Do you like it?"

"Well," said Mrs. Ransome, "it's a little strange. But I like the space."

"Yes, it's a great space. A brilliant space."

Mrs. Ransome hadn't quite meant that but she was not unfamiliar with the concept of space as they talked about space a lot in the afternoons, how people needed it, how they had to be given it and how it had not to be trespassed on.

"She did the place up," he said, "then of course she moved in."

"So you felt," said Mrs. Ransome (and the phrase might have been her first faltering steps in Urdu it seemed so strange on her lips), "you felt that she had invaded your space."

He pointed one beautiful foot at her in affirmation.

"She did. She did. I mean take that fucking pram . . ."

"I remember those," said Mrs. Ransome.

"Yes, well, sure, only *apparently*," he said, "though it wasn't apparent to me, that is not there as a pram. It is there as an object. And it had to be just on that fucking spot. And because I, like, happened to move it, like half an inch, madam went ballistic. Threatened to take everything away. Leave the place bare. As if I cared. Anyway, she's history."

Since she was in Peru Mrs. Ransome felt that she was geography too, a bit, but she didn't say so. Instead she nodded and said, "Men have different needs."

"You're right."

"Are you hurting?" Mrs. Ransome said.

"I was hurting," the young man said, "only now I'm stepping back from it. I think you have to."

Mrs. Ransome nodded sagely.

"Was she upset?" she asked, and she longed to take hold of his foot.

"Listen," he said, "this woman was always upset." He stared out of the window.

"When did she leave you?"

"I don't know. I lose track of time. Three months, four months ago."

"Like February?" said Mrs. Ransome. And it wasn't a question.

"Right."

"Hanson, Ransome," she said. "They're not really alike but I suppose if you're from Peru . . ."

He didn't understand, as why should he, so she told him, told him the whole story, beginning with them coming back from the opera, and the police and the trek out to Aylesbury, the whole tale.

When she'd finished, he said, "Yeah, that sounds like Paloma. It's the kind of thing she would do. She had a funny sense of humor. That's South America for you."

Mrs. Ransome nodded, as if any gaps in this account of events could be put down to the region and the well-known volatility of its inhabitants; the spell of the pampas, the length of the Amazon, llamas, piranha fish—compared with phenomena like these what was a mere burglary in North London? Still, one question nagged.

"Who'd she have got to do it with such care?" Mrs. Ransome asked.

"Oh, that's easy. Roadies."

"Roadies?" said Mrs. Ransome. "Do you mean navvies?"

"A stage crew. Guys who do setups. Picked the lock. Took the photographs. Dismantled your setup, put it up again in Aylesbury. Designer job probably. They're doing it all the time one way or another. No problem, nothing too much trouble . . . provided you pay extra." He winked. "Anyway," he said, looking around the sparsely furnished room, "it wouldn't be such a big job. Is your place like this?"

"Not exactly," Mrs. Ransome said. "Ours is . . . well . . . more complicated."

He shrugged. "She could pay. She was rich. Anyway," he said, getting up from the sofa and taking her hand, "I'm sorry you've been inconvenienced on my account."

"No," said Mrs. Ransome. "It was well, you know, kind of weird to begin with but I've tried to be positive about it. And I think I've grown, you know."

They were standing by the pram.

"We had one of these once," Mrs. Ransome said. "Briefly." It was something she had not spoken of for thirty years.

"A baby?"

"He was going to be called Donald," Mrs. Ransome said, "but he never got that far."

Unaware that a revelation had been made the young man stroked his nipple reflectively as he walked her out into the hall.

"Thank you for clearing up the mystery," she said and (the boldest thing she had ever done in her life) touched him lightly on his bare hip. She was prepared for him to flinch but he didn't, nor was there any change in his demeanor, which was still smiling and relaxed. Except that he also must have thought something out of the ordinary was called for because, taking her hand, he raised it to his lips and kissed it.

One afternoon a few weeks later Mrs. Ransome was coming into Naseby Mansions with her shopping when she saw a van outside and crossing the downstairs lobby she met a young man with a cavalier's hat on and wearing a horse collar round his neck. He was pushing a pram.

"Is he going?" she asked the young man.

"Yeah." He leaned on the pram. "Again."

"Does he move often?"

"Look, lady. This guy moves house the way other people move their bowels. All this"—and he indicated the pram, the horse collar and the cavalier's hat—"is getting the elbow. We're going Chinese now, apparently."

"Let me help you with that," Mrs. Ransome said, taking the pram as he struggled to get it through the door. She wheeled it down the ramp, rocking it slightly as she waited while he disposed the other items inside the van.

"A bit since you pushed one of those," he said as he took it off her. She perched with her shopping on the wall by the entrance, watching as he packed blankets round the furniture, wondering if he was one of the roadies who had moved them. She had not told Mr. Ransome how the burglary had come to pass. It was partly because he would have made a fuss, would have insisted on going up to the top floor to have a word with the young man personally. ("Probably in on it too," he would have said.) It was a meeting Mrs. Ransome had not been able to contemplate without embarrassment. As the van drove off she waved, then went upstairs.

End of story, or so Mrs. Ransome thought, except that one Sunday afternoon a couple of months later Mr. Ransome suffered a stroke. Mrs. Ransome was in the kitchen stacking the dishwasher and hearing a bump went in and found her husband lying on the floor in front of the bookcase, a cassette in one hand, a dirty photograph in the other, and *Salmon on Torts* open on the floor. Mr. Ransome was conscious but could neither speak nor move.

Mrs. Ransome did all the right things, placing a cushion under his head and a rug over his body before ringing the ambulance. She hoped that even in his stricken state her efficiency and self-possession would impress her prostrate husband, but looking down at him while she was waiting to be connected to the appropriate service, she saw in his eyes no sign of approval or gratitude, just a look of sheer terror.

Powerless to draw his wife's attention to the cassette clutched in his hand, or even to relinquish it, her helpless husband watched as Mrs. Ransome briskly collected up the photographs, something at the very back of his mind registering how little interest or surprise was occasioned by this tired old smut. Lastly (the klaxon of the ambulance already audible as it raced by the park) she knelt beside him and prized the cassette free of his waxen fingers before popping it matter-of-factly into her apron pocket. She held his hand for a second (still bent to the shape of the offending cassette) and thought that perhaps the look in his eyes was now no longer terror but had turned to shame; so she smiled and squeezed his hand, saying, "It's not important," at which point the ambulance men rang the bell.

Mr. Ransome has not come well out of this narrative; seemingly impervious to events he has, unlike his wife, neither changed nor grown in stature. Owning a dog might have shown him in a better light, but handy though Naseby Mansions was for the park, to be cooped up in a flat is no life for a dog; a hobby would have helped, a hobby other than Mozart, that is, the quest for the perfect performance only serving to emphasize Mr. Ransome's punctiliousness and general want of warmth. No, to learn to take things as they come he would have been better employed in the untidier arts, photography, say, or painting watercolors; a family would have been untidy too, and, though it seems it was only Mrs. Ransome who felt the loss of baby Donald (and though Mr. Ransome would have been no joke as a father) a son might have knocked the corners off him a little and made life messier—tidiness and order now all that mattered to him in middle age. When you come down to it, what he is being condemned for here is not having got out of his shell, and had there been a child there might have been no shell.

Now he lies dumb and unmoving in Intensive Care and "shell" seems to describe it pretty well. Somewhere he can hear his wife's voice, near but at the same time distant and echoing a little as if his ear was a shell too and he a creature in it. The nurses have told Mrs. Ransome that he can certainly hear what she is saying, and thinking that he may not survive not so much the stroke as the shame and humiliation that attended it, Mrs. Ransome concentrates on clearing that up first. If we can get on a more sensible footing in the sex department, she thinks, we may end up regarding this stroke business as a blessing.

So, feeling a little foolish that the conversation must of necessity be wholly one-sided, Mrs. Ransome begins to talk to her inert husband, or rather, since there are other patients in the ward, murmur in his ear so that from the corner of his left eye Mr. Ransome's view of her is just the slightly furry powdered slope of her well-meaning cheek.

She tells him how she has known about what she calls "his silliness" for years and that there is nothing to feel ashamed of, for it's only sex after all. Inside his shell Mr. Ransome is trying to think what "ashamed" is, and even "feeling" he's no longer quite sure about, let alone "sex"; words seem to have come unstuck from their meanings. Having been sensible about Mr. Ransome's silliness just about brings Mrs. Ransome to the end of her emotional vocabulary; never having talked about this kind of thing much leaves her for a moment at a loss for words. Still, Mr. Ransome, though numb, is at the same time hurting and they plainly need to talk. So, holding his limp hand lightly in hers, Mrs. Ransome begins to whisper to him in that language which she can see now she was meant to acquire for just this sort of eventuality.

"I find it hard to verbalize with you, Maurice," she begins. "We've always found it hard to verbalize with each other, you and me, but we are going to learn, I promise." Pressing her lips up against his unflinching ear she sees in close-up the stiff little gray hairs he regularly crops with the curved scissors during his locked sessions in the bathroom. "The nurses tell me you will learn to talk again, Maurice, and I will learn along with you, we will learn to talk to one another together." The words swirl around his ear, draining into it uncomprehended. Mrs. Ransome speaks slowly. It is like spooning pap into the mouth of a baby; as one wipes the mouth of the untaken food so Mrs. Ransome can almost wipe the ear clean of the curd of the unheeded words.

Still, and she deserves credit for this, she persists.

"I'm not going to be, you know, judgmental, Maurice, because I personally have nothing to be judgmental about." And she tells him how she too has secretly listened to the cassette.

"But in future, Maurice, I suggest we listen to it together, make it a part of honing up on our marital skills . . . because at the end of the day, love, marriage is about choices and to get something out of it you have to put something in."

Out it tumbles, the once tongue-tied Mrs. Ransome now possessed of a whole lexicon of caring and concern which she pours into her husband's ear. She talks about perspectives and sex and how it can go on joyful and un-restrained until the very brink of the grave and she ad-umbrates a future of which this will be a part and how once he gets back on his feet they will set aside quality time which they will devote to touching one another.

"We have never hugged, Maurice. We must hug one another in the future."

Festooned as he is with tubes and drains and moni-tors, hugging Mr. Ransome ill is no easier than hugging Mr. Ransome well, so Mrs. Ransome contents herself with kissing his hand. But having shared with him her vi-sion of the future—tactile, communicative, convivial—she now thinks to top it off with some *Così*. It might just do the trick, she thinks.

So, careful not to dislodge any other of Mr. Ransome's many wires, which are not channels of entertainment at all, Mrs. Ransome gently positions the earphones on his head. Before slipping the cassette into the player she holds it before his unblinking eyes.

"*Così,*" she articulates. And more loudly, "Mozart?"

She switches it on, scanning her husband's unchanging face for any sign of response. There is none. She turns the volume up a little, but not loud, mezzo forte, say. Mr. Ransome, who has heard the word "Mozart" without knowing whether it is a person or a thing or even an articulated lorry, now cringes motionless before a barrage of sounds that are to him utterly meaningless and that have no more pattern or sense than the leaves on a tree, only the leaves on the tree seem to be the notes and there is someone in the tree (it is Dame Kiri) shrieking. It is baffling. It is terrible. It is loud.

Perhaps it is this last awful realization that Mozart does not make sense, or it is because Mrs. Ransome, finding there is still no response, decides to up the volume yet further, just as a last shot, that the sounds vibrate in Mr. Ransome's ears and it is the vibration that does it; but at any rate something happens in his head, and the frail sac into which the blood has leaked now bursts, and Mr. Ransome hears, louder and more compelling than any music he has ever heard, a roaring in his ears; there is a sudden brief andante, he coughs quietly and dies.

Mrs. Ransome does not immediately notice that the numb hand of her husband is now not even that; and it would be hard to tell from looking at him, or from feeling him even, that anything has happened. The screen has altered but Mrs. Ransome does not know about screens. However since Mozart does not seem to be doing the trick she takes the earphones from her husband's head and it's only as she is disentangling the frivolous wires from the more serious ones that she sees something on the screen is indeed different and she calls the nurse.

Marriage, to Mrs. Ransome, had often seemed a

The Lady in the Van

Good nature, or what is often considered as such,
is the most selfish of all virtues:
it is nine times out of ten mere indolence of disposition.

—William Hazlitt,
"On the Knowledge of Character" (1822)

was in the summer of 1971, when Miss Shepherd and her van had for some months been at a permanent halt opposite my house in Camden Town. I had first come across her a few years previously, stood by her van, stalled as usual, near the convent at the top of the street. The convent (which was to have a subsequent career as the Japanese School) was a gaunt reformatory-like building that housed a dwindling garrison of aged nuns and was notable for a striking crucifix attached to the wall overlooking the traffic lights. There was something about the position of Christ, pressing himself against the grim pebble dash beneath the barred windows of the convent, that called up visions of the Stalag and the searchlight and which had caused us to dub him "The Christ of Colditz." Miss Shepherd, not looking uncrucified herself, was standing by her vehicle in an attitude with which I was to become very familiar, left arm extended with the palm flat against the side of the van indicating ownership, the right arm summoning anyone who was fool enough to take notice of her, on this occasion me. Nearly six foot, she was a commanding figure, and would have been more so had she not been kitted out in greasy raincoat, orange skirt, Ben Hogan golfing cap and carpet slippers. She would be going on sixty at this time.

She must have prevailed on me to push the van as far as Albany Street, though I recall nothing of the exchange. What I do remember was being overtaken by two policemen in a panda car as I trundled the van across Gloucester Bridge; I thought that, as the van was certainly holding up the traffic, they might have lent a hand. They were wiser than I knew. The other feature of this first run-in with Miss Shepherd was her driving technique. Scarcely had I put my shoulder to the back of the van, an old Bedford, than a long arm was stretched elegantly out of the driver's window to indicate in textbook fashion that she (or rather I) was moving off. A few yards further on, as we were about to turn into Albany

Street, the arm emerged again, twirling elaborately in the air to indicate that we were branching left, the movement done with such boneless grace that this section of the Highway Code might have been choreographed by Petipa with Ulanova at the wheel. Her "I am coming to a halt" was less poised, as she had plainly not expected me to give up pushing and shouted angrily back that it was the other end of Albany Street she wanted, a mile further on. But I had had enough by this time and left her there, with no thanks for my trouble. Far from it. She even climbed out of the van and came running after me, shouting that I had no business abandoning her, so that passers-by looked at me as if I had done some injury to this pathetic scarecrow. "Some people!" I suppose I thought, feeling foolish that I'd been taken for a ride (or taken her for one) and cross that I'd fared worse than if I'd never lifted a finger, these mixed feelings to be the invariable aftermath of any transaction involving Miss Shepherd. One seldom was able to do her a good turn without some thoughts of strangulation.

It must have been a year or so after this, and so some time in the late sixties, that the van first appeared in Gloucester Crescent. In those days the street was still a bit of a mixture. Its large semi-detached villas had originally been built to house the Victorian middle class, then it had gone down in the world, and, though it had never entirely decayed, many of the villas degenerated into rooming houses and so were among the earliest candidates for what is now called "gentrification" but which was then called "knocking through." Young professional couples, many of them in journalism or television, bought up the houses, converted them and (an invariable feature of such conversions) knocked the basement rooms together to form a large kitchen/dining room. In the mid-sixties I wrote a BBC TV series, *Life in NW1,* based on one such family, the Stringalongs, whom Mark Boxer then took over to people a cartoon strip in the *Listener,* and who kept cropping up in his drawings for the rest of his life. What made the social setup funny was the disparity between the style in which the new arrivals found themselves able to live and their progressive opinions: guilt, put simply, which today's gentrifiers are said famously not to feel (or "not to have a problem about"). We did have a problem, though I'm not sure we were any better for it. There was a gap between our social position and our social obligations. It was in this gap that Miss Shepherd (in her van) was able to live.

October 1969. When she is not in the van Miss S. spends much of her day sitting on the pavement in Parkway, where she has a pitch outside Williams & Glyn's Bank. She sells tracts, entitled "True View: Mattering Things," which she writes herself, though this isn't something she will admit. "I sell them, but so far as the authorship is concerned I'll say they are anonymous and that's as far as I'm prepared to go." She generally chalks the gist of the current pamphlet on the pavement, though with no attempt at artistry. "St. Francis FLUNG money from him" is today's message, and prospective customers have to step over it to get into the bank. She also makes a few coppers selling pencils. "A gentleman came the other day and said that the pencil he had bought from me was the best pencil on the market at the present time. It lasted him three months. He'll be back for another one shortly." D., one of the more conventional neighbors (and not a knocker-through), stops me and says, "Tell me, is she a *genuine* eccentric?"

April 1970. Today we moved the old lady's van. An obstruction order has been put under the windscreen wiper, stating that it was stationed outside number 63 and is a danger to public health. This order, Miss S. insists, is a statutory order: "And statutory means standing—in this case standing outside number 63—so, if the van is moved on, the order will be invalid." Nobody ventures to argue with this, but she can't decide whether her next pitch should be outside number 61 or further on. Eventually she decides there is "a nice space" outside 62 and plumps for that. My neighbor Nick Tomalin and I heave away at the back of the van, but while she is gracefully indicating that she is moving off (for all of the fifteen feet) the van doesn't budge. "Have you let the hand brake off?" Nick Tomalin asks. There is a pause. "I'm just in the process of taking it off." As we are poised for the move, another Camden Town eccentric materializes, a tall, elderly figure in long overcoat and homburg hat, with a distinguished gray mustache and in his buttonhole a flag for the Primrose League. He takes off a grubby canary glove and leans a shaking hand against the rear of the van (OLU246), and when we have moved it forward the few statutory feet he puts on his glove again, saying,

moving slowly round her immobile home, thoughtfully touching up the rust from a tiny tin of primrose paint, looking, in her long dress and sun hat, much as Vanessa Bell would have looked had she gone in for painting Bedford vans. Miss S. never appreciated the difference between car enamel and ordinary gloss paint, and even this she never bothered to mix. The result was that all her vehicles ended up looking as if they had been given a coat of badly made custard or plastered with scrambled egg. Still, there were few occasions on which one saw Miss Shepherd genuinely happy and one of them was when she was putting paint on. A few years before she died she went in for a Reliant Robin (to put more of her things in). It was actually yellow to start with, but that didn't save it from an additional coat, which she applied as Monet might have done, standing back to judge the effect of each brushstroke. The Reliant stood outside my gate. It was towed away earlier this year, a scat-

can lean over and bang on the side of the van, presumably to flush out for his grinning girlfriend the old witch who lives there. I shout at him and he sounds his horn and roars off. Miss S. of course wants the police called, but I can't see the point, and indeed around five this morning I wake to find two policemen at much the same game, idly shining their torches in the windows in the hope that she'll wake up and enliven a dull hour of their beat. Tonight a white car reverses dramatically up the street, screeches to a halt beside the van, and a burly young man jumps out and gives the van a terrific shaking. Assuming (hoping, probably) he would have driven off by the time I get outside, I find he's still there, and ask him what the fuck he thinks he's doing. His response is quite mild. "What's up with you then?" he asks. "You still on the telly? You nervous? You're trembling all over." He then calls me a fucking cunt and drives off. After all that, of course, Miss S. isn't in the van at all, so I end up as usual more furious with her than I am with the lout.

These attacks, I'm sure, disturbed my peace of mind more than they did hers. Living in the way she did, every day must have brought such cruelties. Some of the stall-holders in the Inverness Street market used to persecute her with medieval relish—and children too, who both in-flict and suffer such casual cruelties themselves. One night two drunks systematically smashed all the windows of the van, the flying glass cutting her face. Furious over any small liberty, she was only mildly disturbed by this. "They may have had too much to drink by mistake," she said. "That does occur through not having eaten, possi-bly. I don't want a case." She was far more interested in "a ginger feller I saw in Parkway in company with Mr. Khrushchev. Has he disappeared recently?"

But to find such sadism and intolerance so close at hand began actively to depress me, and having to be on the alert for every senseless attack made it impossible to work. There came a day when, after a long succession of such incidents, I suggested that she spend at least the nights in a lean-to at the side of my house. Initially reluctant, as with any change, over the next two years she gradually abandoned the van for the hut.

In giving her sanctuary in my garden and landing myself with a tenancy that went on eventually for fifteen years I was never under any illusion that the impulse was purely charitable. And of course it made me furious that I had been driven to such a pass. But I wanted a quiet life as much as, and possibly more than, she did. In the garden she was at least out of harm's way.

October 1973. I have run a lead out to the lean-to and now regularly have to mend Miss S.'s electric fire, which she keeps fusing by plugging too many appliances into the attachment. I sit on the steps fiddling with the fuse while she squats on her haunches in the hut. "Aren't you cold? You could come in here. I could light a candle and then it would be a bit warmer. The toad's been in once or twice. He was in here with a slug. I think he may be in love with the slug. I tried to turn it out and it got very disturbed. I thought he was going to go for me." She complains that there is not enough room in the shed and suggests I get her a tent, which she could then use to store some of her things. "It would only be three feet high and by rights ought to be erected in a meadow. Then there are these shatterproof greenhouses. Or something could be done with old raincoats possibly."

March 1974. The council are introducing parking restrictions in the Crescent. Residents' bays have been provided and yellow lines drawn up the rest of the street. To begin with, the workmen are very understanding, painting the yellow line as far as the van, then beginning again on the other side so that technically it is still legally parked. However, a higher official has now stepped in and served a removal order on it, so all this week there has been a great deal of activity as Miss S.

transports cargoes of plastic bags across the road, through the garden and into the hut. While professing faith in divine protection for the van, she is prudently clearing out her belongings against its possible removal. A notice she has written declaring the council's action illegal twirls idly under the windscreen wiper. "The notice was served on a Sunday. I believe you can serve search warrants on a Sunday but nothing else, possibly. I should have the Freedom of the Land for the good articles I've sold on the economy." She is particularly concerned about the tires of the van which "may be miraculous. They've only been pumped up twice since 1964. If I get another vehicle"—and Lady W. is threatening to buy her one—"I'd like them transferred."

The old van was towed away in April 1974 and another one provided by Lady W. ("a titled Catholic lady," as Miss S. always referred to her). Happy to run to a new (albeit old) van, Lady W. was understandably not anxious to have it parked outside her front door and eventually, and perhaps by now inevitably, the van and Miss S. ended up in my garden. This van was roadworthy, and Miss S. insisted on being the one to drive it through the gate into the garden, a maneuver which once again enabled her to go through her full repertoire of hand signals. Once the van was on site Miss S. applied the hand brake with such determination that, like Excalibur, it could never thereafter be released, rusting so firmly into place that when the van came to be moved ten years later it had to be hoisted over the wall by the council crane.

This van (and its successor, bought in 1983) now occupied a paved area between my front door and the garden gate, the bonnet of the van hard by my front step, its rear door, which Miss S. always used to get in and out of, a few feet from the gate. Callers at the house had to squeeze past the back of the van and come down the side, and while they waited for my door to be opened they would be scrutinized from behind the murky windscreen by Miss Shepherd. If they were unlucky, they would find the rear door open with Miss S. dangling her large white legs over the back. The interior of the van, a midden of old clothes, plastic bags and half-eaten food, was not easy to ignore, but should anyone Miss S. did not know venture to speak to her she would promptly tuck her legs back and wordlessly shut the door. For the first few years of her sojourn in the garden I would try and explain to mystified callers how this situation had arisen, but after a while I ceased to care, and when I didn't mention it nor did anyone else.

At night the impression was haunting. I had run a cable out from the house to give her light and heating, and through the ragged draperies that hung over the windows of the van a visitor would glimpse Miss S.'s spectral figure, often bent over in prayer or lying on her side like an effigy on a tomb, her face resting on one hand, listening to Radio 4. Did she hear any movements she would straightaway switch off the light and wait, like an animal that has been disturbed, until she was sure the coast was clear and could put the light on again. She retired early and would complain if anyone called or left late at night. On one occasion Coral Browne was coming away from the house with her husband, Vincent Price, and they were talking quietly. "Pipe down," snapped the voice from the van, "I'm trying to sleep." For someone who had brought terror to millions it was an unexpected taste of his own medicine.

December 1974. Miss S. has been explaining to me why the old Bedford (the van not the music hall) ceased to go, "possibly." She had put in some of her homemade petrol, based on a recipe for petrol substitute she read about several years ago in a newspaper. "It was a spoonful of petrol, a gallon of water and a pinch of something you could get in every High Street. Well, I got it into my head, I don't know why, that it was bicarbonate of soda, only I think I was mistaken. It must be either sodium chloride or sodium nitrate, only I've since been told sodium chloride is salt and the man in Boots wouldn't sell me the other, saying it might cause explosions. Though I think me being an older person he knew I would be more responsible. Though not all old ladies perhaps."

February 1975. Miss S. rings, and when I open the door she makes a beeline for the kitchen stairs. "I'd like to see you. I've called several times. I wonder whether I can use the toilet first." I say I think this is pushing it a bit. "I'm not pushing it at all. I just will do the interview better if I can use the toilet first." Afterwards she sits down in her green mac and purple head scarf, the knuckles of one large mottled hand resting on the clean, scrubbed table and explains how she has devised a method of "getting on the wireless." I was to ask the BBC to give me a phone-in program ("something someone like you could get put on in a jiffy") and then she would ring me up from the house. "Either that or I could get on *Petticoat Line*. I know a darn sight more on moral matters than most of them. I could sing my song over the telephone. It's a lovely song, called 'The End of the World' " (which is pure *Beyond the Fringe*). "I won't commit myself to singing it—not at this moment—but I probably would. Some sense should be said and knowledge known. It could all be anonymous. I could be called The Lady Behind the Curtain. Or A Woman of Britain. You could take a *nom-de-plume* view of it." This idea of The Woman Behind the Curtain has obviously taken her fancy and she begins to expand on it, demonstrating where the curtain could be, her side of it coincidentally taking in the television and the easy chair. She could be behind the curtain, she explains, do her periodic broadcasts, and the rest of the time "be a guest at the television and take in some civilization. Perhaps there would be gaps filled with nice classical music. I know one: Prelude and 'Liebestraum' by Liszt. I believe he was a

some years ago, and my aunt, herself spotless, said I was the cleanest of my mother's children, particularly in the unseen places." I never fathomed her toilet arrangements. She only once asked me to buy her toilet rolls ("I use them to wipe my face"), but whatever happened in that department I took to be part of some complicated arrangement involving the plastic bags she used to hurl from the van every morning. When she could still manage stairs she did very occasionally use my loo, but I didn't encourage it; it was here, on the threshold of the toilet, that my charity stopped short. Once when I was having some building work done (and was, I suppose, conscious of what the workmen were thinking), I very boldly said there was a smell of urine. "Well, what can you expect when they're raining bricks down on me all day? And then I think there's a mouse. So that would make a cheesy smell, possibly."

Miss S.'s daily emergence from the van was highly dramatic. Suddenly and without warning the rear door would be flung open to reveal the tattered draperies that masked the terrible interior. There was a pause, then through the veils would be hurled several bulging plastic sacks. Another pause, before slowly and with great caution one sturdy slippered leg came feeling for the floor before the other followed and one had the first sight of the day's wardrobe. Hats were always a feature: a black railwayman's hat with a long neb worn slightly on the skew so that she looked like a drunken signalman or a French guardsman of the 1880s; there was her Charlie Brown pitcher's hat; and in June 1977 an octagonal straw table-mat, tied on with a chiffon scarf and a bit of cardboard for the peak. She also went in for green eye-shades. Her skirts had a telescopic appearance, as they had often been lengthened many times over by the simple expedient of sewing a strip of extra cloth around the hem, though with no attempt at matching. One skirt was made by sewing several orange dusters together.

When she fell foul of authority she put it down to her clothes. Once, late at night, the police rang me from Tunbridge Wells. They had picked her up on the station, thinking her dress was a nightie. She was indignant. "Does it look like a nightie? You see lots of people wearing dresses like this. I don't think this style can have got to Tunbridge Wells yet."

Miss S. seldom wore stockings, and alternated between black pumps and brown carpet slippers. Her hands and feet were large, and she was what my grandmother would have called "a big-boned woman." She was middle-class and spoke in a middle-class way, though her querulous and often resentful demeanor tended to obscure this; it wasn't a gentle or a genteel voice. Running through her vocabulary was a streak of schoolgirl slang. She wouldn't say she was tired, she was "all done up"; petrol was "juice"; and if she wasn't keen on doing something she'd say "I'm darned if I will." All her conversation was impregnated with the vocabulary of her peculiar brand of Catholic fanaticism ("the dire importance of justice deeds"). It was the language of the leaflets she wrote, the "possibly" with which she ended so many of her sentences an echo of the "Subject to the Roman Catholic Church in her rights etc." with which she headed every leaflet.

May 1976. I have had some manure delivered for the garden and, since the manure heap is not far from the van, Miss S. is concerned that people passing might think the smell is coming from there. She wants me to put a notice on the gate to the effect that the smell is the manure, not her. I say no, without adding, as I could, that the manure actually smells much nicer.

I am working in the garden when Miss B., the social worker, comes with a boxful of clothes. Miss S. is reluctant to open the van door, as she is listening to *Any Answers,* but eventually she slides on her bottom to the door of the van and examines the clothes. She is unimpressed.

MISS S.: I only asked for one coat.

MISS B.: Well, I brought three just in case you wanted a change.

MISS S.: I haven't got room for three. Besides, I was planning to wash this coat in the near future. That makes four.

MISS B.: This is my old nursing mac.

MISS S.: I have a mac. Besides, green doesn't suit me. Have you got the stick?

MISS B.: No. That's being sent down. It had to be made specially.

MISS S.: Will it be long enough?

MISS B.: Yes. It's a special stick.

MISS S.: I don't want a special stick. I want an ordinary stick. Only longer. Does it have a rubber thing on it?

When Miss B. has gone, Miss S. sits at the door of

the van slowly turning over the contents of the box like a chimpanzee, sniffing them and holding them up and muttering to herself.

June 1976. I am sitting on the steps mending my bike when Miss S. emerges for her evening stroll. "I went to Devon on Saturday," she said. "On this frisbee." I suppose she means freebie, a countrywide concession to pensioners that BR ran last weekend. "Dawlish I went to. People very nice. The man over the loudspeaker called us Ladies and Gentlemen, and so he should. There was one person shouted, only he wasn't one of us—the son of somebody, I think." And almost for the first time ever she smiled, and said how they had all been bunched up trying to get into this one carriage, a great crowd, and how she had been hoisted up. "It would have made a film," she said. "I thought of you." And she stands there in her grimy raincoat, strands of lank gray hair escaping from under her head scarf. I am thankful people had been nice to her, and wonder what the carriage must have been like all that hot afternoon. She then tells me about a program on Francis Thompson she'd heard on the wireless, how he had tried to become a priest but had felt he had failed in his vocation, and had become a tramp. Then, unusually, she told me a little of her own life, and how she tried to become a nun on two occasions, had undergone instruction as a novice, but was forced to give it up on account of ill health, and that she had felt for many years that she had failed. But that this was wrong, and it was not a failure. "If I could have had more modern clothes, longer sleep and better air, possibly, I would have made it."

"A bit of a spree," she called her trip to Dawlish. "My spree."

June 1977. On this day of the Jubilee, Miss S. has stuck a paper Union Jack in the cracked back window of the van. It is the only one in the Crescent. Yesterday she was wearing a head scarf and pinned across the front of it a blue Spontex sponge fastened at each side with a large safety pin, the sponge meant to form some kind of peak against the (very watery) sun. It looked like a favor worn by a medieval knight, or a fillet to ward off evil spirits. Still, it was better than last week's effort, an Afrika Korps cap from Lawrence Corner: Miss Shepherd—Desert Fox.

September 1979. Miss S. shows me a photograph she has taken of herself in a cubicle at Waterloo. She is very low in the frame, her mouth pulled down, the photo looking as if it has been taken after death. She is very pleased with it. "I don't take a good photograph usually. That's the only photograph I've seen looks anything like me." She wants two copies making of it. I say that it would be easier for her to go back to Waterloo and do two more. No—that would "take it out of her." "I had one taken in France once when I was twenty-one or twenty-two. Had to go into the next village for it. I came out cross-eyed. I saw someone else's photo on their bus pass and she'd come out looking like a nigger. You don't want to come out like a nigger if you can help it, do you?"

June 1980. Miss S. has gone into her summer rig: a raincoat turned inside out, with brown canvas panels and a large label declaring it the Emerald Weatherproof. This is topped off with a lavender chiffon scarf tied round a sun visor made from an old cornflakes packet. She asks me to do her some shopping. "I want a small packet of Eno's, some milk and some jelly babies. The jelly babies aren't urgent. Oh and, Mr. Bennett, could you get me one of those little bottles of whisky? I believe Bell's is very good. I don't drink it—I just use it to rub on."

August 1980. I am filming, and Miss S. sees me leaving early each morning and returning late. Tonight her scrawny hand comes out with a letter marked "Please consider carefully":

An easier way for Mr. Bennett to earn could be possibly with my cooperative part. Two young men could follow me in a car, one with a camera to get a funny film like "Old Mother Riley Joins Up" possibly. If the car stalls they could then push it. Or they could go on the buses with her at a distance. Comedy happens without trying sometimes, or at least an interesting film covering a Senior Citizen's use of the buses can occur. One day to Hounslow, another to Reading or Heathrow. The bus people ought to be pleased, but it might need their permission. Then Mr. Bennett could put his feet up more and rake it in, possibly.

October 1980. Miss S. has started hankering after a caravan trailer and has just missed one she saw in *Exchange and Mart:* "little net curtains all round, three bunks." "I wouldn't use them all, except," she says ominously, "to put things on. Nice little windows—£275. They said it was sold, only they may have thought I was just

height added to their burdens, put them under some strain. Hence, though she was in sympathy with Mr. Heath on everything except the Common Market, "I do think that Mr. Wilson, personally, may have seen better in regard to Europe, being on the Opposition bench with less salary and being older, smaller and under less strain." She was vehemently opposed to the Common Market—the "common" always underlined when she wrote about it on the pavement, as if it were the sheer vulgarity of the economic union she particularly objected to. Never very lucid in her leaflets, she got especially confused over the EEC. "Not long ago a soul wrote, or else was considering writing [she cannot recall as to which and it may have been something of either], that she disassociated from the Common Market entry and the injustices feared concerning it, or something like that." "Enoch," as she invariably called Mr. Powell, had got it right, and she wrote him several letters telling him so, but in the absence of a wholly congenial party she founded her own, the Fidelis Party. "It will be a party caring for Justice (and as such not needing opposition). Justice in the world today with its gigantic ignorant conduct requires the rule of a Good Dictator, possibly."

Miss S. never regarded herself as being at the bottom of the social heap. That place was occupied by "the desperate poor"—i.e., those with no roof over their heads. She herself was "a cut above those in dire need," and one of her responsibilities in society she saw as interceding for them and for those whose plight she thought Mrs. Thatcher had overlooked. Could it be brought to her attention (and she wrote Mrs. T. several letters on the subject), alleviation would surely follow.

Occasionally she would write letters to other public figures. In August 1978 it was to the College of Cardinals, then busy electing a Pope. "Your Eminences. I would like to suggest humbly that an older Pope might be admirable. Height can count towards knowledge too probably." However this older (and hopefully taller) Pope she was recommending might find the ceremony a bit of a trial, so, ever the expert on headgear, she suggests that "at the Coronation there could be a not so heavy crown, of light plastic possibly or cardboard for instance."

February 1981. Miss S. has flu, so I am doing her shopping. I wait every morning by the side window of the van and, with the dark interior and her grimy hand holding back the tattered purple curtain, it is as if I am at the confessional. The chief items this morning are ginger nuts ("very warming") and grape juice. "I think this is what they must have been drinking at Cana," she says as I hand her the bottle. "Jesus wouldn't have wanted them rolling about drunk, and this is nonalcoholic. It wouldn't do for everyone, but in my opinion it's better than champagne."

October 1981. The curtain is drawn aside this morning and Miss S., still in what I take to be her nightclothes, talks of "the discernment of spirits" that enabled her to sense an angelic presence near her when she was ill. At an earlier period, when she had her pitch outside the bank, she had sensed a similar angelic presence, and now, having seen his campaign leaflet, who should this turn out to be, "possibly," but Our Conservative Candidate Mr. Pasley-Tyler. She embarks on a long disquisition on her well-worn theme of age in politics. Mrs. Thatcher is too young and travels too much. Not like President Reagan. "You wouldn't catch him making all those U-turns round Australia."

January 1982. "Do you see he's been found, that American soldier?" This is Colonel Dozo, kidnapped by the Red Brigade and found after a shoot-out in a flat in Padua. "Yes, he's been found," she says triumphantly, "and I know who found him." Thinking it unlikely she has an acquaintance in the Italian version of the SAS, I ask whom she means. "St. Anthony of course. The patron saint of lost things. St. Anthony of Padua." "Well," I want to say, "he didn't have far to look."

May 1982. As I am leaving for Yorkshire, Miss S.'s hand comes out like the Ancient Mariner's: do I know if there are any steps at Leeds Station? "Why?" I ask warily, thinking she may be having thoughts of camping on my other doorstep. It turns out she just wants somewhere to go for a ride, so I suggest Bristol. "Yes, I've been to Bristol. On the way back I came through Bath. That looked nice. Some beautifully parked cars." She then recalls driving her reconditioned army vehicles and taking them up to Derbyshire. "I did it in the war," she says. "Actually I overdid it in the war," and somehow that is the thin end of the wedge that has landed her up here, yearning for travel on this May morning forty years later.

"Land" is a word Miss S. prefers to "country." "This land . . ." Used in this sense, it's part of the rhetoric if not of madness at any rate of obsession. Jehovah's Witnesses talk of "this land," and the National Front. Land is country plus destiny—country in the sight of God. Mrs. Thatcher talks of "this land."

February 1983. A. telephones me in Yorkshire to say that the basement is under three inches of water, the boiler having burst. When told that the basement has been flooded, Miss S.'s only comment is "What a waste of water."

April 1983. "I've been having bad nights," says Miss S., "but if I were elected I might have better nights." She wants me to get her nomination papers so that she can stand for Parliament in the coming election. She would be the Fidelis Party candidate. The party, never very numerous, is now considerably reduced. Once she could count on five votes but now there are only two, one of whom is me, and I don't like to tell her I'm in the SDP.

Still, I promise to write to the town hall for nomination papers. "There's no kitty as yet," she says, "and I wouldn't want to do any of the meeting people. I'd be no good at that. The secretaries can do that (you get expenses). But I'd be very good at voting—better than they are, probably."

May 1983. Miss S. asks me to witness her signature on the nomination form. "I'm signing," she says: "are you witnessing?" She has approached various nuns to be her nominees. "One sister I know would have signed but I haven't seen her for some years and she's got rather confused in the interim. I don't know what I'll do about leaflets. It would have to be an economy job—I couldn't run to the expense. Maybe I'll just write my manifesto on the pavement; that goes round like wildfire."

May 1983. Miss S. has received her nomination papers. "What should I describe myself as?" she asks through the window slit. "I thought Elderly Spinster, possibly. It also says Title. Well, my title is"—and she laughs one of her rare laughs—"Mrs. Shepherd. That's what some people call me out of politeness. And I don't deny it. Mother Teresa always says she's married to God. I could say I was married to the Good Shepherd, and that's what it's to do with, Parliament, looking after the flock. When I'm elected, do you think I shall have to live in Downing Street or could I run things from the van?"

I speak to her later in the day and the nomination business is beginning to get her down. "Do you know anything about the Act of 1974? It refers to disqualifications under it. Anyway, it's all giving me a headache. I think there may be another election soon after this one, so it'll have been good preparation anyway."

June 1984. Miss S. has been looking in *Exchange and Mart* again and has answered an advert for a white Morris Minor. "It's the kind of car I'm used to—or I used to be used to. I feel the need to be mobile." I raise the matter of a license and insurance, which she always treats as tiresome formalities. "What you don't understand is that I am insured. I am insured in heaven." She claims that since she had been insured in heaven there has not been a scratch on the van. I point out that this is less to do with the celestial insurance than with the fact that the van is parked the whole time in my garden. She concedes that when she was on the road the van did used to get the occasional knock. "Somebody came up behind me once and scratched the van. I wanted him to pay something—half a crown I think it was. He wouldn't."

October 1984. Some new stair carpet fitted today. Spotting the old carpet being thrown out, Miss S. says it would be just the thing to put on the roof of the van to deaden the sound of rain. This exchange comes just as I am leaving for work, but I say that I do not want the van festooned with bits of old carpet—it looks bad enough as it is. When I come back in the evening I find half the carpet remnants slung over the roof. I ask Miss S. who has put them there, as she can't have done it herself. "A friend," she says mysteriously. "A well-wisher." Enraged, I pull down a token piece but the majority of it stays put.

April 1985. Miss S. has written to Mrs. Thatcher applying for a post in "the Ministry of Transport advisory, to do with drink and driving and that." She also shows me the text of a letter she is proposing to send to the Argentinian Embassy on behalf of General Galtieri. "What he doesn't understand is that Mrs. Thatcher isn't the Iron Lady. It's me."

To Someone in Charge of Argentina. 19 April 1985

Dear Sir,

I am writing to help mercy towards the poor general who led your forces in the war actually as a person of true knowledge more than might be. I was concerned with Justice, Love and, in a manner of speaking, I was in the war, as it were, shaking hands with your then leader, welcoming him in spirit (it may have been to do with love of Catholic education for Malvinas for instance) greatly meaning kindly negotiators etc. . . . but I fear that he may have thought it was Mrs. Thatcher welcoming him in that way and it may hence have unduly influenced him.

Therefore I beg you to have mercy on him indeed. Let him go, reinstate him, if feasible. You may read publicly this letter if you wish to explain mercy etc.

I remain.

Yours truly

A Member of the Fidelis Party

(Servants of Justice)

P.S. Others may have contributed to undue influence also.

P.P.S. Possibly without realizing it.

Translate into Argentinian if you shd wish.

Sometime in 1980 Miss S. acquired a car, but before she'd managed to have more than a jaunt or two in it ("It's a real goer!") it was stolen and later found stripped and abandoned in the basement of the council flats in

Maiden Lane. I went to collect what was left ("though the police may require it for evidence, possibly") and found that even in the short time she'd had the Mini she'd managed to stuff it with the usual quota of plastic bags, kitchen rolls and old blankets, all plentifully doused in talcum powder. When she got a Reliant Robin in 1984 it was much the same, a second wardrobe as much as a second car. Miss Shepherd could afford to splash out on these vehicles because being parked in the garden meant that she had a permanent address, and so qualified for full social security and its various allowances. Since her only outgoings were on food, she was able to put by something and had an account in the Halifax and quite a few savings certificates. Indeed I heard people passing say, "You know she's a millionaire," the inference being no one in their right mind would let her live there if she weren't.

Her Reliant saw more action than the Mini, and she would tootle off in it on a Sunday morning, park on

Primrose Hill ("The air is better"), and even got as far as Hounslow. More often than not, though, she was happy (and I think she was happy then) just to sit in the Reliant and rev the engine. However, since she generally chose to do this first thing on Sunday morning, it didn't endear her to the neighbors. Besides, what she described as "a lifetime with motors" had failed to teach her that revving a car does not charge the battery, so that when it regularly ran down I had to take it out and recharge it, knowing full well this would just mean more revving. ("No," she insisted, "I may be going to Cornwall next week, possibly.") This recharging of the battery wasn't really the issue: I was just ashamed to be seen delving under the bonnet of such a joke car.

March 1987. The nuns up the road—or, as Miss S. always refers to them, "the sisters"—have taken to doing some of her shopping. One of them leaves a bag on the back step of the van this morning. There are the inevitable ginger nuts, and several packets of sanitary towels. I can see these would be difficult articles for her to ask me to get, though to ask a nun to get them would seem quite hard for her too. They form some part of her elaborate toilet arrangements, and are occasionally to be seen laid drying across the soup-encrusted electric ring. As the postman says this morning, "The smell sometimes knocks you back a bit."

May 1987. Miss S. wants to spread a blanket over the roof (in addition to the bit of carpet) in order to deaden the sound of the rain. I point out that within a few weeks it will be dank and disgusting. "No," she says—"weather-beaten."

She has put a Conservative poster in the side window of the van. The only person who can see it is me.

This morning she was sitting at the open door of the van and as I edge by she chucks out an empty packet of Ariel. The blanket hanging over the pushchair is covered in washing powder. "Have you spilt it?" I inquire. "No," she says crossly, irritated at having to explain the obvious. "That's washing powder. When it rains, the blanket will get washed." As I work at my table now I can see her bending over the pushchair, picking at bits of soap flakes and redistributing them over the blanket. No rain is at the moment forecast.

June 1987. Miss S. has persuaded the social services to allocate her a wheelchair, though what she's really set her heart on is the electric version.

MISS S.: That boy over the road has one. Why not me?

ME: He can't walk.

MISS S.: How does he know? He hasn't tried.

ME: Miss Shepherd, he has spina bifida.

MISS S.: Well, I was round-shouldered as a child. That may not be serious now, but it was quite serious then. I've gone through two wars, an infant in the first and not on full rations, in the ambulances in

the second, besides being failed by the ATS. Why
should old people be disregarded?

Thwarted in her ambition for a powered chair, Miss S.
compensated by acquiring (I never found out where
from) a second wheelchair ("in case the other conks
out, possibly"). The full inventory of her wheeled vehicles now read: one van; one Reliant Robin; two wheelchairs; one folding pushchair; one folding (two-seater)
pushchair. Now and again I would thin out the pushchairs by smuggling one onto a skip. She would put
down this disappearance to children (never a favorite),
and the number would shortly be made up by yet another wheelie from Reg's junk stall. Miss S. never mas-
tered the technique of self-propulsion in the wheelchair
because she refused to use the inner handwheel ("I can't
be doing with all that silliness"). Instead, she preferred
to punt herself along with two walking sticks, looking in
the process rather like a skier on the flat. Eventually I

ALAN BENNETT

had to remove the handwheel ("The extra weight affects my health").

July 1987. Miss S. (bright-green visor, purple skirt, brown cardigan, turquoise fluorescent ankle socks) punts her way out through the gate in the wheelchair in a complicated maneuver which would be much simplified did she just push the chair out, as well she can. A passer-by takes pity on her, and she is whisked down to the market. Except not quite whisked, because the journey is made more difficult than need be by Miss S.'s refusal to take her feet off the ground, so the Good Samaritan finds himself pushing a wheelchair continually slurred and braked by these large, trailing, carpet-slippered feet. Her legs are so thin now the feet are as slack and flat as those of a camel.

Still, there will be one moment to relish on this, as on all these journeys. When she had been pushed back from

184

the market, she will tell (and it is tell: there is never any thanks) whoever is pushing the chair to leave her opposite the gate but on the crown of the road. Then, when she thinks no one is looking, she lifts her feet, pushes herself off, and freewheels the few yards down to the gate. The look on her face is one of pure pleasure.

October 1987. I have been filming abroad. "When you were in Yugoslavia," asks Miss S., "did you come across the Virgin Mary?" "No," I say, "I don't think so." "Oh, well, she's appearing there. She's been appearing there every day for several years." It's as if I've missed the major tourist attraction.

January 1988. I ask Miss S. if it was her birthday yesterday. She agrees guardedly. "So you're seventy-seven." "Yes. How did you know?" "I saw it once when you filled out the census form." I give her a bottle of whisky, explaining that it's just to rub on. "Oh. Thank you."

Pause. "Mr. Bennett. Don't tell anybody." "About the whisky?" "No. About my birthday." Pause. "Mr. Bennett." "Yes?" "About the whisky either."

March 1988. "I've been doing a bit of spring cleaning," says Miss S., kneeling in front of a Kienholz-like tableau of filth and decay. She says she has been discussing the possibility of a bungalow with the social worker, to which she would be prepared to contribute "a few hundred or so." It's possible that the bungalow might be made of asbestos, "but I could wear a mask. I wouldn't mind that, and of course it would be much better from the fire point of view." Hands in mittens made from old socks, a sanitary towel drying over the ring, and a glossy leaflet from the Halifax offering "fabulous investment opportunities."

April 1988. Miss S. asks me to get Tom M. to take a photograph of her for her new bus pass. "That would make a comedy, you know—sitting on a bus and your bus pass out of date. You could make a fortune out of that with very little work involved, possibly. I was a born tragedian," she says, "or a comedian possibly. One or the other anyway. But I didn't realize it at the time. Big feet." She pushes out her red, unstockinged ankles. "Big hands." The fingers stained brown. "Tall. People trip over me. That's comedy. I wish they didn't, of course. I'd like it easier, but there it is. I'm not suggesting you do it," she says hastily, feeling perhaps she's come too near self-revelation, "only it might make people laugh." All of this is said with a straight face and no hint of a smile, sitting in the wheelchair with her hands pressed between her knees and her baseball cap on.

May 1988. Miss S. sits in her wheelchair in the road, paintpot in hand, dabbing at the bodywork of the Reliant, which she will shortly enter, start, and rev for a contented half hour before switching off and paddling down the road in her wheelchair. She has been nattering at Tom M. to mend the clutch, but there are conditions. It mustn't be on Sunday, which is the feast of St. Peter and St. Paul and a day of obligation. Nor can it be the following Sunday apparently, through the Feast of the Assumption falling on the Monday and being transferred back to the previous day. Amid all the chaos of her life and now, I think, more or less incontinent, she trips with fanatical precision through this liturgical minefield.

September 1988. Miss S. has started thinking about a flat again, though not the one the council offered her a few years ago. This time she has her eye on something much closer to home. My home. We had been talking outside, and I left her sitting on the step in the hall while I came back to work. This is often what happens: me sitting at my table, wanting to get on, Miss S. sitting outside rambling. This time she goes on talking about the flat, solilo-quizing almost, but knowing that I can hear. "It need only be a little flat, even a room possibly. Of course, I can't manage stairs, so it would have to be on the ground floor. Though I'd pay to have a lift put in." (Louder.) "And the lift wouldn't be wasted. They'd have it for their old age. And they'll have to be thinking about their old age quite soon." The tone of it is somehow familiar from years ago. Then I realize it's like one of the meant-to-be-overheard soliloquies of Richmal Crompton's William.

Her outfit this morning: orange skirt, made out of three or four large dusters; a striped blue satin jacket; a green head scarf—blue eye shield topped off by a khaki peaked cap with a skull-and-crossbones badge and Rambo across the peak.

February 1989. Miss S.'s religion is an odd mixture of traditional faith and a belief in the power of positive thinking. This morning, as ever, the Reliant battery is running low and she asks me to fix it. The usual argument takes place:

ME: Well, of course it's run down. It will run down unless you run the car. Revving up doesn't charge it. The wheels have to go round.

MISS S.: Stop talking like that. This car is not the same. There are miracles. There is faith. Negative thoughts don't help. (*She presses the starter again and it coughs weakly.*) There, you see. The devil's heard you. You shouldn't say negative things.

The interior of the van now indescribable.

March 1989. Miss S. sits in the wheelchair trying to open the sneck of the gate with her walking stick. She tries it with one end, then reverses the stick and tries with the other. Sitting at my table, trying to work, I watch her idly, much as one would watch an ant trying to get round some obstacle. Now she bangs on the gate to attract the attention of a passerby. Now she is wailing. Banging and wailing. I go out. She stops wailing, and explains she has her washing to do. As I maneuver her through the gate, I ask her if she's fit to go. Yes, only she will need help. I explain that I can't push her there. (Why can't I?) No, she doesn't want that. Would I just push her as far as the corner? I do so. Would I just push her a bit further? I explain that I can't take her to the launderette. (And anyway there is no launderette anymore, so which launderette is she going to?) Eventually, feeling like Fletcher Christian (only not Christian) abandoning Captain Bligh, I leave her in the wheelchair outside Mary H.'s. Someone will come along. I would be more ashamed if I did not feel, even when she is poorly, that she knows exactly what she's about.

March 1989. There is a thin layer of talcum powder around the back door of the van and odd bits of screwed up tissues smeared with what may or may not be shit, though there is no doubt about the main item of litter, which is a stained incontinence pad. My method of re-trieving these items would not be unfamiliar at Sellafield. I don rubber gloves, put each hand inside a plastic bag as an additional protection, then, having swept the fecal ar-tifacts together, gingerly pick them up and put them in the bin. "Those aren't all my rubbish," comes a voice from the van. "Some of them blow in under the gate."

April 1989. Miss S. has asked me to telephone the social services, and I tell her that a social worker will be call-ing. "What time?" "I don't know. But you're not going to be out. You haven't been out for a week." "I might be. Miracles do happen. Besides, she may not be able to talk to me. I may not be at the door end of the van. I might be at the other end." "So she can talk to you there." "And what if I'm in the middle?"

Miss C. thinks her heart is failing. She calls her Mary. I find this strange, though it is of course her name.

27 April 1989. A red ambulance calls to take Miss S. to the day center. Miss B. talks to her for a while in the van, gradually coaxing her out and into the wheelchair, shit streaks over her swollen feet, a piece of toilet roll clinging to one scaly ankle. "And if I don't like it," she keeps asking, "can I come back?" I reassure her, but, looking at the inside of the van and trying to cope with the stench, I find it hard to see how she can go on living here much longer. Once she sees the room they are offering her, the bath, the clean sheets, I can't imagine her wanting to come back. And indeed she makes more fuss than usual about locking the van door, which suggests she accepts that she may not be returning. I note how, with none of my distaste, the ambulance driver bends over her as he puts her on the hoist, his careful rearrangement of her greasy clothing, pulling her skirt down over her knees in the interests of modesty. The chair goes on the hoist, and slowly she rises and comes into view above the level of the garden wall and is wheeled into the ambulance. There is a certain distinction about her as she leaves, a Dorothy Hodgkin of vagabonds, a derelict Nobel Prize winner, the heavy folds of her grimy face set in a kind of resigned satisfaction. She may even be enjoying herself.

When she has gone I walk round the van noting the occasions of our battle: the carpet tiles she managed to smuggle onto the roof, the blanket strapped on to muffle the sound of the rain, the black bags under the van stuffed with her old clothes—sites of skirmishes all of which I'd lost. Now I imagine her bathed and bandaged and cleanly clothed and starting a new life. I even see myself visiting and taking flowers.

This fantasy rapidly fades when around 2:30 Miss S. reappears, washed and in clean clothes, it's true, and with a long pair of white hospital socks over her shrunken legs, but obviously very pleased to be back. She has a telephone number where her new friends can be contacted, and she gives it to me. "They can be reached," she says, "any time—even over the holiday. They're on a long-distance bleep."

As I am leaving for the theater, she bangs on the door of the van with her stick. I open the door. She is lying wrapped in clean white sheets on a quilt laid over all the accumulated filth and rubbish of the van. She is still worrying that I will have her taken to hospital. I tell her there's no question of it and that she can stay as long as she wants. I close the door, but there is another bang and I reassure her again. Once more I close the door, but she bangs again. "Mr. Bennett." I have to strain to hear. "I'm sorry the van's in such a state. I haven't been able to do any spring cleaning."

28 April. I am working at my table when I see Miss B. arrive with a pile of clean clothes for Miss Shepherd, which must have been washed for her at the day center yesterday. Miss B. knocks at the door of the van, then opens it, looks inside and—something nobody has ever done before—gets in. It's only a moment before she comes out, and I know what has happened before she rings the bell. We go back to the van where Miss Shepherd is dead, lying on her left side, flesh cold, face gaunt, the neck stretched out as if for the block, and a bee buzzing round her body.

It is a beautiful day, with the garden glittering in the sunshine, strong shadows by the nettles, and bluebells out under the wall, and I remember how in her occasional moments of contemplation she would sit in the wheelchair and gaze at the garden. I am filled with remorse for my harsh conduct towards her, though I know at the same time that it was not harsh. But still I never quite believed or chose to believe she was as ill as she was, and I regret too all the questions I never asked her. Not that she would have answered them. I have a strong impulse to stand at the gate and tell anyone who passes.

Miss B. meanwhile goes off and returns with a nice doctor from St. Pancras who seems scarcely out of her teens. She gets into the van, takes the pulse in Miss S.'s outstretched neck, checks her with a stethoscope and, to save an autopsy, certifies death as from heart failure. Then comes the priest to bless her before she is taken to the funeral parlor, and he, too, gets into the van—the third person to do so this morning, and all of them without distaste or ado in what to me seem three small acts of heroism. Stooping over the body, his bright white hair brushing the top of the van, the priest murmurs an inaudible prayer and makes a cross on Miss S.'s hands and head. Then they all go off and I come inside to wait for the undertakers.

I have been sitting at my table for ten minutes before I realize that the undertakers have been here all the time, and that death nowadays comes (or goes) in a gray Ford transit van that is standing outside the gate. There are three undertakers, two young and burly, the third older and more experienced—a sergeant, as it were, and two corporals. They bring out a rough gray-painted coffin, like a prop a conjuror might use, and, making no comment on the surely extraordinary circumstances in which they find it, put a sheet of white plastic bin-liner over the body and manhandle it into their magic box, where it falls with a bit of a thud. Across the road, office workers stroll down from the Piano Factory for their lunch, but nobody stops or even looks much, and the Asian woman who has to wait while the box is carried over the pavement and put in the (other) van doesn't give it a backward glance.

Later I go round to the undertakers to arrange the funeral, and the manager apologizes for their response when I had originally phoned. A woman had answered, saying, "What exactly is it you want?" Not thinking callers rang undertakers with a great variety of requests, I was nonplussed. Then she said briskly, "Do you want someone taken away?" The undertaker explains that her seemingly unhelpful manner was because she thought my call wasn't genuine. "We get so many hoaxes these days. I've often gone round to collect a corpse only to have it open the door."

9 *May*. Miss Shepherd's funeral is at Our Lady of Hal, the Catholic church round the corner. The service has been slotted into the ten o'clock mass, so that, in addition to a contingent of neighbors, the congregation includes what I take to be regulars: the fat little man in thick glasses and trainers who hobbles along to the church every day from Arlington House; several nuns, among them the ninety-nine-year-old sister who was in charge when Miss S. was briefly a novice; a woman in a green straw hat like an upturned plant pot who eats toffees throughout; and another lady who plays the harmonium in tan slacks and a tea-cozy wig. The server, a middle-aged man with white hair, doesn't wear a surplice, just ordinary clothes with an open-necked shirt,

priest turns out to have a good strong voice, though its tone is more suited to "Kum Ba Ya" than to Newman and J. B. Dykes. The service itself is wet and wandering, even more so than the current Anglican equivalent, though occasionally one catches in the watered-down language a distant echo of 1662. Now, though, arrives the bit I dread, the celebration of fellowship, which always reminds me of the warm-up Ned Sherrin insisted on inflicting on the studio audience before *Not So Much a Programme,* when everyone had to shake hands with their neighbor. But again the nice man who fetched us the prayer books shames me when he turns round without any fuss or embarrassment and smilingly shakes my hand. Then it is the mass proper, the priest distributing the wafers to the ninety-nine-year-old nun and the lady with the plant pot on her head, as Miss S. lies in her coffin at his elbow. Finally there is another hymn, this one by the (to me) unknown hymnodist Kevin Norton, who's obviously reworked it from his unsuccessful entry for

the Eurovision Song Contest; and with the young priest
acting as lead singer, and the congregation a rather sub-
dued backing group, Miss Shepherd is carried out.

The neighbors, who are not quite mourners, wait on
the pavement outside as the coffin is hoisted onto the
hearse. "A cut above her previous vehicle," remarks
Colin H.; and comedy persists when the car accompany-
ing the hearse to the cemetery refuses to start. It's a familiar scene, and one which I've played many times,
with Miss S. waiting inside her vehicle as well-wishers
lift the bonnet, fetch leads and give it a jump start. Except this time she's dead.

Only A. and I and Clare, the ex-nurse who lately be-
friended Miss S., accompany the body, swept around
Hampstead Heath at a less than funereal pace, down
Bishop's Avenue and up to the St. Pancras Cemetery,
green and lush this warm, sunny day. We drive beyond
the scattered woods to the furthest edge where stand
long lines of new gravestones, mostly in black polished

the nuns, that it was the death of her fiancé in this inci-
dent that "tipped her over." It would be comforting to
think that it is love, or the death of it, that unbalances
the mind, but I think her early attempts to become a
nun and her repeated failures ("too argumentative," one
of the sisters said) point to a personality that must already have been quite awkward when she was a girl.
After the war she spent some time in mental hospitals,
but regularly absconded, finally remaining at large long
enough to establish her competence to live unsuper-
vised.

The turning point in her life came when, through no
fault of hers, a motorcyclist crashed into the side
of her van. If her other vans were any guide, this one
too would only have been insured in heaven, so it's not
surprising she left the scene of the accident ("skedad-
dled," she would have said) without giving her name or
address. The motorcyclist subsequently died, so that,
while blameless in the accident, by leaving the scene

of it she had committed a criminal offense. The police mounted a search for her. Having already changed her first name when she became a novice, now under very different circumstances she changed her second and, calling herself Shepherd, made her way back to Camden Town and the vicinity of the convent where she had taken her vows. And though in the years to come she had little to do with the nuns, or they with her, she was never to stray far from the convent for the rest of her life.

All this I learned in those last few days. It was as if she had been a character in Dickens whose history has to be revealed and her secrets told in the general setting-to-rights before the happy-ever-after, though all that this amounted to was that at long last I could bring my car into the garden to stand now where the van stood all those years.

Postscript (1994)

This account of Miss Shepherd condenses some of the many entries to do with her that are scattered through my diaries. Unemphasized in the text (though deducible from the dates of the entries) is the formality of her last days. The Sunday before she died she attended mass, which she had not done for many months; on the Wednesday morning she allowed herself to be taken to be bathed and given clean clothes and then put to bed in the van on clean sheets; and that same night she died. The progression seemed so neat that I felt, when I first wrote it up, that to emphasize it would cast doubt on the truth of my account, or at least make it seem sentimental or melodramatic. However, the doctor who pronounced Miss Shepherd dead said that she had known other deaths in similar circumstances; that it was not (as I had facetiously wondered) the bath that had killed her but that to allow herself to be washed and put into clean clothes was both a preparation and an acknowledgment that death was in the offing.

Nor is it plain from the original account how in the period after her death I got to know the facts of her life that she had so long concealed. A few months before, a bout of flu must have made her think about putting her affairs in order and she had shown me an envelope that I might need "in case anything happens to me, possibly." I would find the envelope in the place under the banquette where she kept her savings books and other papers. What the envelope contained she did not say, and, when in due course she got over the flu and struggled on, nothing more was said about it.

It was about this time, though, that I had the first and only hint that her name might not be her own. She had, I knew, some money in the Abbey National, and periodically their bright brochures would come through my door—young and happy homeowners pictured gaily striding across their first threshold and entering upon a life of mortgaged bliss.

"Some post, Miss Shepherd," I would knock on the window and wait for the scrawny hand to come out (nails long and gray; fingers ocher-stained as if she had been handling clay). The brochure would be drawn back into the dim and fetid interior, where it would be a while before it was opened, the packet turned over and over in her dubious hands, the Society's latest exciting offer waiting until she was sure it was not from the IRA. "Another bomb, possibly. They've heard my views."

In 1988 the Abbey National were preparing to turn themselves from a building society into a bank, a proposal to which Miss Shepherd for some reason (novelty, possibly) was very much opposed. Before filling in her ballot form, she asked me (and she was careful to couch the question impersonally) if a vote would be valid had the purchaser of the shares changed their name. I said, fairly obviously, that if the shares had been bought in one name then it would be in order to vote in that name. "Why?" I asked. But I should have known better, and, as so often, having given a teasing hint of some revelation, she refused to follow it up, just shook her head mutely, and snapped shut the window. Except (and this was standard procedure too) as I was passing the van next day her hand came out.

"Mr. Bennett. What I said about change of name, don't mention it to anybody. It was just in theory, possibly."

For some days after Miss Shepherd's death I left the van as it was, not from piety or anything to do with decorum but because I couldn't face getting into it, and though I put on a new padlock I made no attempt to extract her bank books or locate the necessary envelope. But the news had got round, and when one afternoon I came home to find a scrap dealer nosing about I realized I had to grit my teeth (or hold my nose) and go through Miss Shepherd's possessions.

To do the job properly would have required a team of archaeologists. Every surface was covered in layers of old clothes, frocks, blankets and accumulated papers, some of them undisturbed for years and all lying under a crust of ancient talcum powder. Sprinkled impartially over wet slippers, used incontinence pads and half-eaten tins of baked beans, it was of a virulence that supplemented rather than obliterated the distinctive odor of the van. The narrow aisle between the two banks of seats where Miss Shepherd had knelt, prayed and slept was trodden six inches deep in sodden debris, on which lay a topdressing of old food, Mr. Kipling cakes, wrinkled apples, rotten oranges and everywhere batteries—batteries loose, batteries in packets, batteries that had split and oozed black gum onto the prehistoric sponge cakes and ubiquitous sherbet lemons that they lay among. A handkerchief round my face, I lifted one of the banquettes where in the hollow beneath she had told me her bankbooks were hidden. The underside of the seat was alive with moths and maggots, but the books were there, together with other documents she considered valuable: an MoT certificate for her Reliant, long expired; a receipt for some repairs to it done three years before; an offer of a fortnight of sun and sea in the Seychelles that came with some car wax. What there was not was the envelope. So there was nothing for it but to excavate the van, to go through the festering debris in the hope of finding the note she had promised to leave, and with it perhaps her history.

Searching the van, I was not just looking for the envelope; sifting the accumulated refuse of fifteen years, I was hoping for some clue as to what it was that had happened to make Miss Shepherd want to live like this. Except that I kept coming across items that suggested that living "like this" wasn't all that different from the way people ordinarily lived. There was a set of matching kitchen utensils, for instance—a ladle, a spatula, a masher for potatoes—all of them unused. They were the kind of thing my mother bought and hung up in the kitchen, just for show, while she went on using the battered old-faithfuls kept in the knife drawer. There were boxes of cheap soap and, of course, talcum powder, the cellophane wrapping unbreached; they too had counterparts in the dressing-table drawer at home. Another item my mother hoarded was toilet rolls, and here were a dozen. There was a condiment set, still in its box. When, amid such chaos, can she have hoped to use that particular appurtenance of gentility? But when did we ever use ours, stuck permanently in the sideboard cupboard in readiness for the social life my parents never had or ever really wanted? The more I labored, the less peculiar the van seemed—its proprieties and aspirations no different from those with which I had been brought up.

There was cash here too. In a bag Miss Shepherd carried round her neck there had been nearly £500, and peeling off the soggy layers from the van floor I collected about £100 more. Taking into account the money in various building societies and her National Savings certificates, Miss Shepherd had managed to save some £6,000. Since she was not entitled to a pension, most of this must have been gleaned from the meager allowance she got from the DHSS. I am not sure whether under the present regime she would have been praised for her thrift or singled out as a sponger. Arch-Tory though she was, she seems a prime candidate for Mr. Lilley's little list, a paid-up member of the Something for Nothing society. I would just like to have seen him tell her so.

Modest though Miss Shepherd's estate was, it was more than I'd been expecting and made the finding of the envelope more urgent. So I went through the old clothes again, this time feeling gingerly in the pockets and shaking out the greasy blankets in a blizzard of moth and "French Fern." But there was nothing, only her bus pass, the grim photograph looking as if it were taken during the siege of Stalingrad and hardly auguring well for the comedy series she had once suggested I write on the subject. I was about to give up, having decided that she must have kept the envelope on her and that it had been taken away with the body, when I came upon it, stiff with old soup and tucked into the glove compartment along with another cache of batteries and sherbet lemons, and marked "Mr. Bennett, if necessary."

Still looking for some explanation ("I am like this, possibly, because . . ."), I opened the envelope. True to form, even in this her final communication Miss Shepherd wasn't prepared to give away any more than she had to. There was just a man's name, which was not her own, and a phone number in Sussex.

I finished cleaning out the van, scraped down the aisle, and opened all the windows and doors so that for the first time since she had moved in it was almost sweet-smelling—only not, because sweet in an awful way was how she had made it smell. My neighbor, the artist David Gentleman, who ten years before had done a lightning sketch of Miss Shepherd watching the removal of an earlier van, now came and did a romantic drawing of this her last vehicle, the grass growing high around it and the tattered curtains blowing in the spring breeze.

2 *May 1989.* This afternoon comes a rather dapper salvage man who, fifteen years ago, refused to execute a council order for the removal of one of Miss Shepherd's earlier vans on the grounds that someone was living in it. So he says anyway, though it's perhaps just to establish his claim. He stands there on the doorstep, maybe waiting to see if I am going to mention a price; I wait too, wondering if he is going to mention a charge. Silence on both sides seems to indicate that the transaction is over with no payment on either side, and within the hour he

He tells me her history and how, returning from Africa just after the war, he found her persecuting their mother, telling her how wicked she was and what she should and shouldn't eat, the upshot being that he finally had his sister committed to a mental hospital in Hayward's Heath. He gives her subsequent history, or as much of it as he knows, saying that the last time he had seen her was three years ago. He's direct and straightforward and doesn't disguise the fact that he feels guilty about having her committed yet cannot see how he could have done otherwise, how they never got on, and how he cannot see how I have managed to put up with her all these years. I tell him about the money, slightly expecting him to change his tune and stress how close they had really been. But not a bit of it. Since they hadn't got on he wants none of it, saying I should have it. When I disclaim it too, he tells me to give it to charity.

Anna Haycraft (Alice Thomas Ellis) had mentioned Miss S.'s death in her *Spectator* column, and I tell him about this, really to show that his sister did have a place in people's affections and wasn't simply a cantankerous old woman. "Cantankerous is not the word," he says, and laughs. I sense a wife there, and after I put the phone down I imagine them mulling over the call.

I mull it over too, wondering at the bold life she has had and how it contrasts with my own timid way of going on—living, as Camus said, slightly the opposite of expressing. And I see how the location of Miss Shepherd and the van in front but to the side of where I write is the location of most of the stuff I write about; that too is to the side and never what faces me.

Over a year later, finding myself near the village in Sussex where Mr. F. lived, I telephoned and asked if I could call. In the meantime I'd written about Miss Shepherd in the *London Review of Books* and broadcast a series of talks about her on Radio 4.

17 June 1990. Mr. and Mrs. F. live in a little bungalow in a modern estate just off the main road. I suppose it was because of the unhesitating fashion in which he'd turned down her legacy that I was expecting something grander; in fact Mrs. F. is disabled and their circumstances are obviously quite modest, which makes his refusal more creditable than I'd thought. From his phone manner I'd been expecting someone brisk and businesslike, but he's a plumpish, jolly man, and both he and his wife are full of laughs. They give me some lovely cake, which he's baked (Mrs. F. being crippled with arthritis), and then patiently answer my questions.

The most interesting revelation is that as a girl Miss S. was a talented pianist and had studied in Paris under Cortot, who had told her she should have a concert career. Her decision to become a nun put an end to the piano, "and that can't have helped her state of mind" says Mr. F.

He recalls her occasional visits, when she would

never come in by the front door but lope across the field at the back of the house and climb over the fence. She never took any notice of Mrs. F., suspecting, rightly, that women were likely to be less tolerant of her than men.

He says all the fiancé stuff, which came via the nuns, is nonsense; she had no interest in men, and never had. When she was in the ambulance service she used to be ribbed by the other drivers, who asked her once why she had never married. She drew herself up and said, "Because I've never found the man who could satisfy me." Mystified by their laughter she went home and told her mother, who laughed too.

Mr. F. has made no secret of the situation to his friends, particularly since the broadcasts, and keeps telling people he's spent his life trying to make his mark and here she is, having lived like a tramp, more famous than he'll ever be. But he talks about his career in Africa, how he still works as a part-time vet, and I come away thinking what an admirable pair they are, funny and kind and as good in practice as she was in theory—the brother Martha to his sister's Mary.

Sometimes now hearing a van door I think, "There's Miss Shepherd," instinctively looking up to see what outfit she's wearing this morning. But the oil patch that marked the site of the van has long since gone, and the flecks of yellow paint on the pavement have all but faded. She has left a more permanent legacy, though, and not only to me. Like diphtheria and Brylcreem, I associate moths with the forties, and until Miss Shepherd took up residence in the drive I thought them firmly confined to the past. But just as it was clothes in which the plague was reputedly spread to the Derbyshire village of Eyam so it was a bundle of Miss Shepherd's clothes, for all they were firmly done up in a black plastic bag, that brought the plague to my house, spreading from the bag to the wardrobe and from the wardrobe to the carpets, the appearance of a moth the signal for frantic clapping and savage stamping. On her death my vigorous cleaning of the van broadcast the plague more widely, so that now many of my neighbors have come to share in this unwanted legacy.

Her grave in the Islington St. Pancras Cemetery is scarcely less commodious than the narrow space she slept in the previous twenty years. It is unmarked, but I think as someone so reluctant to admit her name or divulge any information about herself, she would not have been displeased by that.

ABOUT THE TYPE

This book was set in Caledonia, a typeface designed in 1939 by William Addison Dwiggins for the Mergenthaler Linotype Company. Its name is the ancient Roman term for Scotland, because the face was intended to have a Scotch Roman flavor. Caledonia is considered to be a well-proportioned, businesslike face with little contrast between its thick and thin lines.